THE *Just* MAN

MEL MAE SCHMIDT

The *Just* Man

Translated from the German by

The Translation Smithy

26 | TWENTY SIX

TWENTYSIX – the publishing company for self-publishing
An co-operation between the publishing group of Random House and BoD – Books on Demand
Production and Publishing company: BoD – Books on Demand, Norderstedt, Germany.
Cover design by CC0 Creative Commons, pixabay.com
Cover and inside Illustrations by CC0 Creative Commons, pixabay.com
Quotes in italics by German ecumenical Bible translation
('Unity translation')
German first edition © by Mel Mae Schmidt 2016
Printed and bound in Germany

www.twentysix.de

ISBN: 9783740746544

There was a bad, sharp wind blowing through the woodlands, it howled wildly furious around every housetop. Full of anger it drove every creature half frozen into warm shelter. They crawled under warming foliage or straw for taking cover. The first snowflakes of the year fell slow-moving and they attempted to mollify the furious wind.

But the wild icewind scattered the little innocent flakes and howled spitefully its sounds. Thereupon the flakes fell en masse down from the dark vault and the cold wind enjoyed it to whip them around now all the more furious. With zeal the snowflakes tried to slide down in gentle dance, but the wind was full of anger. Incandescence inflamed his passions and no one could escape him.

He threw the flakes around with huge icecold hands and blew his sharpness at full tilt down to earth. Greedily he blew sharp puffs and everything that's not standing firmly on the ground got swirled up and off.

That evening was star-bright and the emerging frost started to move into the land. Father Frost entered his retreat at silent steps and cloaked everything in his frosty veil, so that onto every surface there were lying a white glittering coat of ice and it was freezing its beneath instantly.

Nothing was spared from him.

The icecold winter took up its quaters.

He shoved aside with his cold hard hand the autumn that would warn the summer against the coming winter for long as well as to prepare him for it.

Now a severe snowstorm was governing and no creature dared to set a foot onto the street, if it hasn't to.

Except the many homeless, whose fate now laid in the icecold hands of the winter and he doubtlessly would suck the life out from their chest one after another and would let them become solidified.

The bright light of the street lamps refracted in all of the many straying snowflakes and caused reflected sparkling light onto the more and more increasing snow cover lying on the streets, roofs and bushes.

The remaining leaves of the trees laid around withered and brown, now covered with white, hither and tither and they illustrated, that life was gone and now the death was dawning. In the new year, life would come back again in all its glory and bloom and it will bring along the fresh and gentle fragrance of the blooming flowers.

Unless this, the death would govern in its icecold coat and it will cause its anthem along with the wild sharp whistling of the frosty wind to herald the start of the new regency, so that all creatures would get to know this lore and may revere the new ruler. A frosty coldness whistled around every cabin and was greedily seeking admittance. If she did not find one, she tried to do it with little grooves or gaps in the masonry to make herself felt. Would it be cold—one begann to freeze—so she knew that she was noticed and she wrapped her arms around this person even tighter.

In one of these cabins there was a just man sitting, and he was reading a book. He was sitting there in his large library in front of his warm fireplace and was burying himself in a book with refreshing heart. Full of passion he was soaking every single word of the reading in and he was so lost in this other world, that he did not notice as with greedy heart the cold found admittance in his cabin through a hatch, slowly starting to embrace him hard.

It seemed, as if all the many books in the shelves would embrace and protect this just man with their lines like a warm blanket made of written words.

Deeper and deeper was the cold digging into the flesh of this just. His body started to shiver and shudder badly and the cold already began to sneer. She added still more coldness to this man, yet he did not stir at all.

The cold was wondering and embraced him tighter and tighter. But it couldn't be helped. Then the cold was frightened at the sight of his heart, which was beating warmly and blissfully in the chest of the man, and let up on him. This heart was that full of kindness, warmth and love, that the cold couln't achieve anything.

'Hello,' quoth the heart to the cold there. 'How are you, my daughter?'

It smiled.

The cold was frightened and was only staring at that

heart, which still smiled kindly at the cold being pure and fine and without any prejudice.

It did not know anything bad, everything evil was foreign to it.

The heart looked at the cold expectanly. But the cold didn't want to respond to it. Everything nice and good was foreign to her.

She turned away without a word and faded away. The heart was only smiling good-naturedly and left it at that.

In fact, it did not often hit society!

The just man did not notice anything of these things by seeming to be lost in his world of books. What a book has to say to him, what it wants him to let him know, the just man listened to it like no other. He could give himself hour after hour to a book, being indulged all over in it and being lost in it.

Just like listening to a good friend he was listening carefully to the many words of the book and he was learning every single word almost greedily that a book could whisper to him with such an abandon, that he nearly lost his heart on it.

The just man—the book whisperer—didn't step outside the house very often, being overfond of spending his time in his library with all his beloved friends, and listening carefully to their tales about foreign countries, cultures and adventures.

On the contrary, if one meets the just man in the street sometime, so this encounter was never in vain; every person he met in passing, he gave a note to take with them with a saying or a good thought written on it.

They were wondering first, but by unfolding this note and finding a good and encouraging sentence on it, so they became overwhelmed with joy and they found this man as good and caring.

And when they were asking for advice or help, they never asked in vain.

Not even if he was once again sitting there with a book and wanted to do something good to himself.

He liked to help.

Always.

Day and night.

When they were knocking on his door, they never

knocked in vain. His big, good heart was endless, his love and helpfulness immeasurable. He was living alone and his gender was neutral. When he just had his books, he was the happiest man on earth. And as long as his heart was pure, he found himself and the world being good.

Especially in the evening — when it started to dawn outside —, the just man was again sitting in his large library onto his big red wing chair in front of the crackling fireplace, and was listening eagerly to the wise words of one of his many eloquently friends, who took him into distant countries to distant cultures and into unknown and new adventures every evening.

Many women were really keen on this just man, but he did not see them. Many men requested his company, but he did not see them. That was not even once meant as an offense, since he always was helping in other respects where needed. But for all that, these people simply were no books. Otherwise the just man would have not hesitated for one second to get their company.

Despite that the just man were rarely going outside, he

had a good reputation. People liked him. The rare cases, in which he set his foot onto the trottoir were always filled with graciousness, kindness and kind words. Pure sympathy were streaming towards him. Not just because he was a wealthy man and didn't hold down a job, but also because his visage was shining with such sympathy, that one had to like him as soon as one caught sight of him.

The just man was possessing a large set of books. His library was crammed full of books of every description from the floor up to the roof. He was mad about reading. Not just did he loved tales—no—he once in a while liked to read non-fiction stories or biographies.

Notwithstanding many a biography was similar to a tale—but a true tale. Nothing bad, immoral, indecent, dissolute or lowbrow was allowed to be in the house of the just man. He was a man of the highest moral and he cultivated his virtues. His mind was only getting something sublime and elevated for nourishment. It did not know of anything rotten.

The just man ensured with caution that only everything

good got into his heart and his mind, and he was contemplating about this and that philosophically before he went to bed every evening.

He was a man of less words, but of many thoughts. Would he actually give tongue to all of his thoughts, his mouth never came to rest. Even at night time he kept himself from sleeping with profound thoughts, and his mind always remained astute and alert.

Day in, day out the just man was in cheerful disposition, because his heart was beating jolly in his chest. How else was it to be then? The heart knew only everything lovely, all the cruelties of the world out there were foreign to that little heart. It did not even sense, that there was another world existing. On top of that, a world of being evil! However, one day, its master – the just man – received a letter.

He opened it and all at once something stabbed through his body. It was a horrible pain, which the heart had never felt before. It could barely breathe, it gasped for breath.

Big burning tears were running down the face of the just

man and so they were smudging the ink of the letter. He had to sit down and put one hand on his heart.

'O good God,' it was breaking out of him full of pain. 'O God!' For the heart all of that was foreign. What was going on here? What did this portend?

The just man blew his nose with a handkerchief and wiped off his tears from his face after an awful passion of tears. His eyes were red, wet and puffy. For many years, the just man hadn't wept yet. 'No, no, no,' the just man was whispering repeatedly. 'No, no no.'

The pain—the little just heart was feeling—didn't ease off. It was stabbing deeper and deeper, more and more burning through its body. A glowing sword was forging ahead through the good heart and this was shaking it so much, that the heart was thinking, it couldn't go on beating no longer.

For all one is worth, the heart tried to go on beating, to keep its master and itself alive, and to go on transporting blood through his body, even if the pain was getting worse and worse. The heart had to control itself not to scream. It was stumbling wildly and it hoped, that the pain would disappear.

Suddenly, the just man fell down on his knees in his book-filled library and was weeping and moaning and he complained sorrowfully. The heart couln't go on any longer. Now it also was screaming.

A burning twinge shot through the heart and was filled with it entirely. The little heart got into a panic. It didn't know, how long it was able to beat, when the pain have it still standing. When it will be extinguished.

The just man fisted severely on the wooden floor and wasn't able to stop his lacrimal lake. He couldn't stop.

Not until a good half-hour has passed, the just man was able to find any peace of mind slowly, and no tear was there any longer - only stunned emptiness. The just man was raising dead slow and in the aftermath of a short stagger he sat down into his big wing chair and was watching the blazing fire in the fireplace.

He was still holding the letter of bringing ill luck in his hand – now totally rumpled and tear-stained. Being weary and weak because of all the tears he cried, the just man

soon fell asleep softly, and his heart — his weary little heart — was able to find any peace of mind slowly, but kept
the burning sword in its body, which was contained in
the letter.

A few days after, the just man was standing in front of
his mirror of the boudoir and stared at himself with red
puffy eyes. He looked down at himself – black.

His entire suit was completely black.

An absolute darkness.

His heart — once being refreshed — was now only a
painful and stunned machine in his chest. It had very
much sorrow, and since that terrible day the letter
arrived at the just man, it only was looking out of dull
eyes.

It didn't feel less like committing suicide, just to stop
pumping. To stop forwarding blood. Just standing still
and extinguishing.

The just man sighed.

Anew, one little teardrop absconded out of one eye and
was hurried running down the cheek, where she first
paused and probably was considering, if she really is
ought to jump. Shortly afterwards she jumped down and
was falling safely onto the suit of the just man.

But he didn't care. Now he didn't care about anything.
He had lost his dearest, he could still call his own on

earth. In a hurry, one's life was able to end. No soul was safe from the icecold hands of the death, no one was able to escape them.

They are snatching after one full of greed and are grasping full of passion, to carry the soul into another world, which is foreign to the earthy one. No fleshly one is ever able to get there, except through death.

Life has to be completed here to continue it elsewhere in another way and in another sphere. This was life. No one ever could escape from it. Who started existing had to continue it.

There was no choice existing, no one had ever been asked about it. At least no one was aware of it. The just man looked at his watch and wiped the tears off his face. He blew his nose.

Outside, the snow was fluttering silently and it laid its soft fingers onto the shoulder of every sad child, man or woman to whisper comfort to them.

Without ado the icecold monarch covered his people with white glance and thus he was stealing into the hearts of his subjects, who were fooled by snow and ice and thereby dominated by them.

The just man took his walking stick, hat, coat and scarf shakily and left the house. No one he ran across, dared to look at the just man or even to approach him. The tidings of the tragic occasions went around fast and one had great compassion with this kind-hearted, merciful, at all times ready to help just man.

* * *

'My condolences,' said a small, slender gentleman, gently shaking the just man's hand. In turn he nodded thankfully. A large number of people stood in line to express their deepest sympathy to the just man. With a numb and heavy heart, he only nodded once in a while and endured it all.

Then—finally—he stood at the closed coffin. Trembling, he laid a hand on it and swallowed hard.

He struggled desperately to retain his composure.

Everyone watched him with a heavy heart.

The just man sobbed and now cried bitterly and leaned

himself upon the coffin with oppressive sorrow.

'No,' he whispered. 'No, no, no, no. It is not true, it cannot and must not be true.'

Loud sobs filled the room.

The people around him looked at each other with sadness and did not know how to help the poor just man. Along with him, his heart also cried in his chest, whose fiery hot stab now burned again and his fiery tongue almost consumed the little heart.

Full of sorrow, the stabbed heart discharged itself into tears and cries and could not find an end. The fire wound that burned itself into the heart was too strong, the numbing and emptiness were too strong.

Never before had the heart experienced such a thing. Such a strong bitterness was alien to him. The cup of sorrow was filled to the brim with black bile. And the little heart had to drink it empty. This is how his master had taught him: 'Do not reject the suffering,' the just man once said, 'for gaining Paradise, first of all hell must be crossed and demons—whose home is our soul—must be defeated. Only when we kill the poisonous, the evil, the rotting, are we allowed to enter clean.'

The funeral went emotionless and numb for the just man. As if from another world, the priest spoke at the grave and looked pityingly upon the just man.

Then the coffin along with the loved one inside were lowered into the grave and buried. The just man watched impassively.

His heart beat exhausted in his chest; tired, burned out, dead. There was not a single tear left to cry. He was completely dry, like the Sahara.

For a long time the just man remained standing at the grave after all the others had left. He didn't want to go to the funeral feast. He didn't see any sense in it. It was as if eating the deceased, especially when he thought of all the different cold cut platter, he was overtaken by terrible disgust.

He looked upon the gravestone for a long time and could not believe that this one special man lay down in the earth.

Lifeless.

Without breath.

Ice cold.

Wondering, what it was like. To be no more?

The just man was blowing his nose. His warm breath steamed within the cold. Until now, the day had been snow-free. But now a few small white flakes were dancing down from the sky. Some of them laid down very gently and mildly on the hat and shoulders of the just man as if they wanted to offer him their condolences and give him their comfort.

Like little cold ghosts they surrounded him and whispered flatteries into his ear.

They spoke of good days, beautiful memories and a good heart.

Nothing was eternal, everything fleeting, but nothing lapsed.

Moments that once had been, were not indifferent with passing. They lived on and in the wind of earthliness they continued to dance their air dances full of bliss.

What seemed to be gone wasn't gone. It just assumed a different shape. As a caterpillar was not gone as soon as it became a butterfly, so the man who dies wasn't gone either, but was now holding a different form in another world.

The snow ghosts, who now performed their dances more numerous and covered the surfaces with white powder, spoke softly.

Now the wind came up and surrounded the just man with its sounds. It grabbed him and shook him. It blew wild noises and dispersed the soft dances of the snowflakes.

The just man sniffed. It was time to go. He would come back. Nothing would change here, the eternal sleep was immutable.

'Farewell,' he spoke and walked through the wild dance of snowflakes and the wind, without turning one last time.

* * *

Arriving home in his library, he sat down exhausted in his wing chair. The fireplace was freshly lit. His housekeeper had quickly turned it on just before she left for a cozy warm home coming.

'So that you are at least physically warm when it is not so psychologically,' she had said and looked out of sad eyes at the just man.

She is so good to me, the just man thought, and only now did he perceive the pleasant scent of cocoa. He looked at the small table next to the wingchair and was utterly amazed to find a large cup of steaming hot chocolate there, as well as biscuits.

Immediately the just man got a blissful feeling. His heart leaped in his chest and rejoiced over something good, no matter how small.

He courageously grabbed the large steaming cup and soaked up the cocoa smell deeply.

He sighed. Then he took a sip. His heart was dancing.

I feel like a little boy, thought the just man.

Life slowly came back to him.

Crazy, what a cup of hot chocolate can achieve, he thought and sipped his cocoa with relish.

He clasped the cup with both hands and a flood of warm bliss filled the just man and tickled his heart.

He took some of the pastry and dipped it briefly into the hot cocoa before eating it.

It did somebody good and not only it warmed the body.

Also the soul, the heart was filled with great joy.

Chocolate was known as Soulflatter. Chocolate comforted, helped, did good.

So he sat there, the just man, and did himself well. Meanwhile, a heavy blizzard raged outside and the just man was glad he hadn't gone to the funeral feast. He would have had to go home in this storm otherwise.

So he just sat in his big wingchair and ate and drank and watched the fire in the fireplace dancing.

He let his mind run free while his heart beat slowly and deliberately in his chest. It enjoyed that the deep pain just subsided and hoped that it would not return so soon.

Indeed, the glowing hot sword continued to sit in the small body of the heart, however it did not move for now and did not tear at the gaping wound.

So the just man sat there quietly with his little heart and lost himself in thoughts. Like being in a trance, he stared into the fire and breathed in and out calmly. He wasn't able to say how long he was sitting there. Time and space lost themselves and became one.

At some point, however, he looked at his watch and was horrified to have sat there for three hours. His stomach growled and demanded a proper meal. His housekeeper had already prepared and warmed everything so that the just man only needed to eat it.

She is much too good to me, he thought to himself, I have to thank her. She cheered me up and comforted me.

After lunch, he went back from the kitchen to the library, where he sat down in the wingchair with one of his best friends and began to disappear into another, better, less gruesome world.

Greedily he began to absorb the words, as he had done as ever.

Although the aching hot sword was still standing across his chest—ready to attack and stab again—life came back into the heart of the just man and he found great comfort in his faithful friends, the books.

Though the just man often lay there at night and cried until his eyes closed with exhaustion, but week after week he became lighter on his heart.

He discovered the chocolate for himself and since that terrible day—when he returned home from the funeral—he drank hot cocoa to his reading.

Hot healing balm lay down on his heart and helped the just man to process what he had been taken.

The little just heart in his chest began to recover and was soon able to jump and laugh again.

The just man now read all the more books during his mourning and the greedier than ever before. Together with the hot chocolate, he had discovered a healing new therapy for himself against depression, and applied it with heart's blood. He was full of praise for his housekeeper about the hot chocolate and thanked her almost daily for her idea to cook some for him.

'My heart thanks you, my dearest,' said the just man, giving his housekeeper a kiss on the hand. She just smiled embarrassed and shouted: 'Oh, you charmer, it's just hot chocolate!' She laughed.

The just man smiled. 'To me, it's redemption.'

* * *

Soon spring would come and turn the icy death into warming life.

Weeks before, the sun showed up more and more often and made the frost of the night melt away. The first birds let their songs sound from trees and rooftops and here and there some insects started humming around.

On a sunny Sunday morning the just man was after a walk.

It was still cold and the breath was still freezing in the icy cold air. Well wrapped up, the hat on his head, the walking stick in his hand, the just man left his house for the first time after weeks. Outside he met all kinds of beautiful things.

Known faces also ran into him. Only with a timid smile did they look at the just man, knowing that he was suffering. They still didn't know how to meet him. Should they smile, greet him? Or would one rather just stare down?

So it was first of all the just man to smile and greet to help all the timid people out of their oppression. And to show — I'm back again. Death did not extinguish my inner fire of life.

When the people saw that the just man was no longer depressed by death and his grief, their faces brightened up considerably and they smiled and greeted him warmly.

The just man felt more alive than he had felt for a long time and his heart jumped refreshed in his chest and rejoiced in life again.

So the just man wandered about in the gentle rays of the sunshine of spring, and soaked everything in he encountered; here a little boy running after his ball screeching and cheering, there an old lady who threw old breadcrumbs at the doves and watched them enthusiastically as they took in the crumbs. Although still freezing cold, the just man breathed in the fresh air deeply. With renewed love for life, he walked through the nearby park and soon settled on a bench. This bench stood under a large tree, whose treetop still had no leaves and thus threw the gentle ray of sunshine through, in the midst of which the just man sat and let the rays affect him. He closed his eyes and lived.

Nothing else. Just existing. Nothing was important anymore, only breathing in and out, just enjoying, the here and now. This one moment. Amidst nature, the beautiful side of the pilgrimage through life. Simply being. In the midst of all the other creatures, each with its own individual style, each one a grain of salt in this world.

The just man opened his eyes again. But at that moment he recognized an elderly gentleman who cowered on a bench on the other side of the park and cried visibly. The just man sighed with compassion. Then he grabbed into the inside of his cloak and fetched out his collection of writings with the little notes that he occasionally slipped

to other people in passing to cheer them up. That was a
long time ago.

He looked at all the notes and finally found what he was
looking for. So the just man stood up and went over to
this poor old man. Standing in front of him, he looked up
with bloodshot eyes. The just man gave him the note
with a gentle smile. Confused, the old man accepted it
and opened it timidly:

*'Accept the fire-heated sword with a joyful
heart out of the hands of life, for
you do not know whether one comes, that is
of a more poisonous nature and is a hundred
times hotter than the current one.'*

The old man looked up speechlessly at the just man and
nodded a 'yes'. He knew about the suffering of the just
man and therefore also that this saying was not an empty
phrase of him.

The just man smiled at the poor old man one last time

and turned to go. On the way back to his bank, he thought about his own line. It was so true. Even if life hits you so hard, who knew whether the next thing that hits you was a hundred times harder? The just man became serious.

He looked – as he sat back on the bench – over to the poor old man. How numb he sat on the bench and appeared like a picture of misery. But he had stopped crying and seemed very thoughtful.

'Be blessed,' the just man whispered and wished this poor sad little man all the best from the bottom of his heart.

Full of compassion, he lowered his head and closed his eyes.

Suddenly, someone briefly touched him on the shoulder and the just man looked up. It was the little man.

He was very surprised. 'Yes, please?' said the just man and smiled heartily.

'Thank you,' said the old man with a timid smile.

The just man kept smiling. 'You are welcome.'

'How can I be good for you?' asked the man.

The just man stopped him with a wave of his hand. 'Just hug a tree with all of your heart and with all your love, and your pain has no longer any power over you.' The just man stood up and took his hat off to say goodbye. He walked away.

Further away, he turned again and saw the little man embracing the tree with deepness, where the just man has left him.

Full of abandon and hope, the man clung to the thick, large tree and awaited a miracle from God.

May it be granted to him, the just man thought with a mild smile and continued on his way.

* * *

When he returned home after almost two hours, he felt fresh and happy.

'Your chocolate is waiting for you,' said the housekeeper, winking at the just man mischievously. He immediately got big eyes like a little boy on Christmas Eve. 'And biscuits?' he wanted to know. The housekeeper laughed.

'Yes, and biscuits, too.'

The just man laughed, too. 'You're a real angel!' Smartly he gave her a big kiss on the cheek, which made her immediately blush. 'You're a rogue.'

The just man smiled. 'A chocolate-addicted rogue, please.' He flashed his pearly-white teeth.

'Well, go ahead with you,' laughed the housekeeper. 'Otherwise your hot love gets cold.'

The just man grinned. 'Yes, ma' am.'

And immediately he disappeared in the library to his friends.

So the accustomed life returned to the just man and the familiar laid down around the stabbed heart like a blissful balm. The nightmares disappeared and the just man regained restful sleep to wake up refreshed to a new morning.

More and more often the sun came up and spring was already over the countryside. The just man had now made it his habit to go for a walk every Sunday morning, and in the afternoon to make himself comfortable with a hot cup of 'love'— as the housekeeper used to say—and with biscuits and a book in his private library.

One Saturday morning, when the just man was poking about in the shops, he witnessed a theft. It was happening that the just man entered a small corner shop, when a customer shouted out: 'He's a thief, he swiped something!' Immediately the salesman was with the thief and held him.

'What did you steal?' The elderly gentleman was the sad little man, the just man recognized and observed how this one produced an apple.

'I'll inform the police,' the salesman replied severely.

The sad little man wore such a terribly snivelling look, that the just man's heart hurt in his chest with compassion. He stepped in between. 'That won't be necessary.'

With certainty he stood in front of the salesman.

This one was slightly smaller than the just man and looked up surprised to him. 'Oh, and why not?'

'Because I will vouch for him,' said the just man. 'I'll pay the apple.'

He pulled out his wallet.

The salesman gave a laugh. 'And you think that's enough? He's still a thief and the police needs to be informed!'

He looked coolly at the just man.

'Are **you** without sin?' This was a trick question.

The seller seemed confused. 'Excuse me?'

'This gentleman,' the just man began, 'is a poor, destitute man who has only recently suffered a blow of fate. He just wants to survive. It did mean no harm. So I ask you: Are you without sin? If so, cast the first stone and inform the police.'

The just man gave the salesman a challenging look.

This one swallowed, looked around at the other

attendants in his shop and at the poor little man, and

then looked again at the just man.

'Well, for my sake. Pay that stupid apple.' The salesman

held out his hand and the just man put enough money

into it.

'Are you now satisfied?' The just man wanted to know

for certainty.

The salesman nodded and growled a 'yes.'

So the just man took the sad little man with him to his

house, fed him, warmed him — for the wind was still

cool — and clothed him.

'Do you have a place to live?' the just man asked and

looked sympathetically at the little weak man as he

shook his head.

'No', he replied. 'That was my stroke of fate. Work gone,

apartment gone. Homeless. Alone.' Bitter tears ran hotly

over his cheeks.

The just man's heart was lacerated at this sight. The hot

sword drew and dragged again in his chest. The little heart cried and screamed. The eyes of the just man were also filled with hot tears and they ran down his cheeks. His compassion was enormous.

He gently took the poor little man's wet face into both hands and he looked at the just man with red, wet and sad eyes. The just man looked at him with similiar eyes and his facial expressions showed painful and infinite compassion. He said: 'My brother, stay with me. You get clothes, food, warmth, a roof over your head and love. With me you will not be deficient in anything and if you do, let me know and I will make you receive everything you need to be happy.' While he was talking, a hot thick tear ran out of his eye. The poor man stared with wide eyes at the just man in disbelief. 'What do you mean, Sir?'

The just man nodded gently smiling. 'You are most welcome. Stay under the protection of my house. You'll be fine.'

The little man could hardly believe it. He was admitted

to this man's house? Never starve again, never freeze again, never be lonely again.

His heart jumped in his chest and he got warm. No tears of sorrow flowed anymore, now tears of joy came forth. The small, poor, slender man began to laugh with tears of joy, and—for that matter—the just man laughed as he cried tears of joy. Both hearts of the two men in their chests laughed and cried. Although the sword was still burning, the heart of the just man jumped in his chest and rejoiced.

'And you are allowed to use my library,' the just man offered to the poor man, pointing to the shelves full of books. 'There must be something for you, too.' The just man winked at the little man with a smile and this one also smiled. 'Thank you very much, Sir.'

At that moment the housekeeper appeared and peeked into the library. 'Oh, you have a visitor? Shall I serve up a little something?' She smiled heartily.

The just man jumped up from his chair in the library while he had offered the little man his beloved wingchair and shouted cheerfully: 'Yes, please! Bring lots of cocoa and biscuits! In particular, we have a permanent guest, he'll be living here from now on.'

The just man smiled mildly at the housekeeper. She looked at the poor, crouching and very shy man and understood immediately. She smiled at him encouraging. 'I'd love to. So 'lots of cocoa' – as you wish,' she laughed and disappeared into the kitchen.

The just man sat down again and said: 'This is my housekeeper. And now yours, too. She is our good soul and very charming.' He smiled gently and winked at the still very reserved and modest man to make things easier for him.

'Have you ever drunk hot chocolate – cocoa?' the just man wanted to know and watched the little man shake his head. 'No,' he whispered, 'never. Never heard of it.' 'Is there such a thing?' the just man said. 'Then you'll be introduced to a wonderful soul flatterer. Our good soul makes us a lot of it. It's really very good for the spirit,' said the just man, and the housekeeper came into the room with a tray of steaming chocolate and biscuits.

'There's a whole pot of cocoa here,' said the housekeeper, 'take all you want. I'd love to cook new one.'

'Thank you, my dearest,' said the just man and the housekeeper disappeared out of the room. The just man gave the little man a cup and then took his own.

'Oh, that smells wonderful,' the little man noticed radiantly and sipped on it. Immediately his eyes shone. 'Oh...,' was all he could say in amazement. Immediately he swallowed a whole sip and was on fire for this drink. The little man looked at the just man in amazement.

'How is that possible? It's like a balm cream for my maltreated soul....' There was another sip.

'Chocolate is good for the soul,' said the just man gently. 'It always helps me. Almost as good as a good psalm. I didn't mean to deny you that.'

The little man greedily drank the healing balm and then took it in. He closed his eyes. The just man sipped on his cup and watched the little man.

'What does it taste like to you?' the just man asked the little man. Silence.

Then the little man opened his eyes. 'Like salvation.'

The just man smiled. 'Yes. For me, too.'

Five

The days passed and the little man settled in better and better with the just man.

In the village it went around, that the just man took in the poor man he had saved from the police, and everyone had great respect for him.

'He's so good,' the patrons said.

'Someday he won't be so good any more,' the enviers said.

The men wanted to meet him now even more for informative conversation and the women wanted to marry him all the more.

The just man didn't care about either. He didn't do good for prestige, for others, not even for heaven. He did good because he **was** good.

Because he couldn't help it. His heart was like that. Good. Since the little man lived with the just man and he wore better clothes now, received regular food and shaved himself with fresh water, he now looked just as respectable as the master of the house himself.

The just man was often seen outside with the little man and people were amazed at the transformation of the poor little man. He looked like the old father of the just man, they were so much alike. They went for a walk in the park, where the little man once lived. They fed the doves, they watched playing children and let the beginning summer sun shine on them. It was wondered, how the just man dealt with the little man in such a way that he called him 'brother' and suchlike.

No one could have known, that the just man meant the 'brother in spirit', that he equated himself with the little man and to be with him on the same level and understood him like a brother, that he addressed him as a kind of soulmate. Likewise, he forbade the little man to continue addressing him with 'Sir' — they should be brothers, equal in position, equal in the spirit, equal in front of the world.

Pure, true love arose between the just man and the little man: they were like brothers to each other.

The little man was deeply grateful to the just man for the transformation of his life. Likewise that the just man taught him his virtues and advised him the purity of heart.

'Meet everyone as you would like to be met. No matter what sacrifice this demands of you, no matter whether the other is your friend, your enemy, a stranger. Stay in peace, do not condemn and do not insult,' the just man once said to the little man, 'because life is a game. It has rules that benefit you and others. If you follow them, you will win. Who wants to lose voluntarily?'

The little man was impressed by the wisdom of the just man.

'Be a light that shines brightly,' the just man smiled mildly at the little man. This one looked at him with wide eyes. He stored in his heart what the just man — his brother — taught him.

Because that was the real life.

'And,' the just man continued, 'always choose the good. In every situation. Even if they hurt you, beat you, insult you, insult your loved ones - don't insult back, don't curse back and don't fight back. But rather bless.'

The little man looked at the just man in confusion. 'But,

my brother... how?'

The just man continued to smile mildly. He put both hands on the shoulder of the little man. 'I know, dear brother, that the easiest thing to do is to pay like with like—that, when you get hurt, you'd like to pay it back in kind, to pay back the same thing that makes you angry. But that's where the mistake is. After all, if you react in the way that a person, who has caused damage, expects it from you - what is special about it? It is better to react unexpectedly for oneself and the other one, and thus to unsettle this other person and at the same time to make peace. When you repay anger with anger, you only get incandescence. And in the end, they're both on fire.' The little man understood and looked admiringly at the just man. 'Living is much better with a light heart,' the just man added with a smile.

Thus the weeks and even months passed and the just man taught the little man everything that was necessary to have a good heart, the only true life. The little man wrote everything down eagerly to read it again and again. The just man and the little man became very big adherents of hot chocolate and indulged themselves abundantly in it every evening.

Life seemed to be not changing its path and no suffering could cloud this heavenly sphere.

Until that day in autumn, when the little man did not wake up one morning. Eternal sleep had carried him away. There was nothing the doctor could do for him. The poor man had died in the end as a just man, with a heart full of love.

The just man felt how the hot long forgotten sword in his chest revived and how hot tears ran down over his cheeks.

He prepared the funeral of the little man especially gorgeously and stood again at a grave, inside of which only lifelessness and coldness reigned.

The heart in the just man's chest shouted with all its might, wept, raged, fought.

The scarred old wound tore open and burned and hurt like never before. The little heart was overwhelmed by this chastisement and had great difficulty not to stand still. Crying and weaping it rushed forward, hurriedly pumping blood through the body of the just man and became more and more exhausted.

This pain, this eternal pain....

* * *

When the just man returned home, he sought comfort in his hot love. Only after hours did he discover a pile of letters lying on his chest of drawers and approached them with a numbed heart.

He was scared.

No! — it passed through him.

He knew the handwriting only too well. These letters came from his love, which he had to carry to her grave at that time. The date said, they were sent the same day she

died.

His love was sick, often and for a long time she stayed in cure. Their mutual love was pure, genuine and honest.

The most daring closeness was her hand in his hand and a hesitant gentle kiss on the forehead.

She was a fragile angel.

Now, where did all the letters come from?

Immediately the just man hurried to the housekeeper.

'They all arrived just as I put them on the dresser, Sir. I don't know what this is all about.'

The just man disappeared spiritlessly into the library.

He hesitated to open the letters. What did it say in there? What might she have left him?

* * *

ON 16TH DECEMBER

So tell me, what can I do? My heart is burning for you, thirsting. The longing is hard to bear, I long for you. In order to be able to en- joy your closeness, which is not yet close enough to me, I acted like being without any feelings, I lied to you so that I could continue to communicate with you. O could you know how much I still thirst for you, how much I desire you in the deepest depths of my soul. How can I satisfy this crude desire for your essence, how can I get your love? What do you want me to do? So tell me how I get through the day without you. Even the very thought of you consumes me. My heart wants YOU!

ON 17TH DECEMBER

It drives me out of my mind when I think of you. Every time I receive a new letter from you, my heart beats like crazy. I don't know if it's that good to continue to be friends with you when I long for you in a much deeper way and it consumes me to be only close to you on this level.

Why don't you want to feel more for me? Why do you want to stay away from me, why don't you want me? I would die for you'but you don't see me. Why don't you feel like I do for you? Please save me from those hot flames of love that burn my heart!

Come to me! Take me in your arms and tell me that everything will be all right, everything will be as I dreamed it would be.

But you're not here. I miss you so much. Whether being in contact or not, my heart refuses to give up on you. It refuses to leave your heart. My heart cries out for you, for your heart. But your heart does not hear, it closes up. How can I mean so much to you that you want my friendship, but still so little that you push my love away from you?

Is it so bad to be able to love me? Is it wrong? Can one love me at all? If you only knew how much you mean to me, how much you fill my heart, there is hardly any room for other things! How can you sleep calmly when I plague myself at night and torture myself with thoughts of you, with loving words on my lips for you.... Oh, sweetheart, how much I miss you. I'd love to tell you, but then you'd go away even further away from me than you do now. Woe betide anyone who tells you and thus aggravates my grief. But I myself can't tell you, too big is the fear of losing you again, as I have done too often. My heart is also tormenting about, when another girl enraptures and enchants you; how my heart could bear it.

Woe to the girl who takes you away from me and you step into her love trap. No one is worthy to get you and yet I want you, O my sweet sun, my happiness, my joy, my one and only!

My heart is dependent on you, you give it vital energy and joie de vivre, a reason to exist. If you left, how could I know my heart was alive, with what kind of magic? It has become weak, it feels your repulsive nature of its longing and love for you. It dries up slowly alive and bends to the ground. Thousand holes and a thousand stings, a thousand wounds and a thousand bites have tortured my heart that loves you to death. And it is ready to endure many more thousands of wounds, bites, stings and holes, even if it ought to die because of it, just for the sake of your love. Death – the loss of one's own heart – weighs nothing compared to what it would be like to wait for an ordinary anatomical cardiac death and have to endure a life without you. Only a kiss from you and all suffering would be blurred, only a hug and a kind word and all wounds would heal.

One step towards me means more to my heart than the eternal waiting for redemption. O if the heart would have its own voice that immediately sounds when it worries, wastes away or rejoices! If there were such a voice, you heard only wailing, crying and weeping at night and during the day... my heart will die without you, it will dry up without your love, which would make me so happy and alive, if you only could love me! Tell me, my sweet delight, what can I do to win your love?

I miss you, my little star. I love you... you 're so faraway from me....

Heaven alone knows when we 'll meet one day. It knows how much I long for you, how many times I 've cried for you and how many tears I 've shed for you.

Please, heart, don 't forget me...

ON 18TH DECEMBER – IN THE MORNING

Remember that I have loved many male beings and no one was granted to stay in my heart for a long time afterwards. Only you have got the boon that one may not forget you, only you are the man whose heart is not one of many, but only YOU. You 're someone one just don 't like to forget. Even the many torments that you have inflicted on me my heart is able to forget, for you are radiant. No matter how many more kicks follow into my heart, this one will always love you, don 't forget that, O sweet bliss.

You may be forgiven and forgotten because you shine brighter than the sun, you are sweeter than honey and more interesting than any yarn in the world. You just can't be hated and forgotten. If that were the case, I would no longer understand the world. My heart cannot do this, for it loves you too much to be angry with you... my love, my life.

On 18th December – In the evening

When you told me that I was like a very good friend to you – a sister – it shredded my heart. No woman wants to hear that from the man she loves. Even if this man doesn't return the woman's love. It's poison. Pure poison. A bloody'painful kick into the heart, whose wounds reappear and a pool of blood flows together. You are careless in your choice of words and your behavior towards a person whose heart gets easily destroyed, whose mind gets easily confused and where the secret longing easily threatens to overwhelm. I silently have tolerated many of your actions and words in the hour of carelessness, for the love of you. Much of it hit me right into my heart, many of it was the outbreak of an avalanche of tears, but I kept telling myself that it doesn't matter, I love you and that's all that matters. Quite true but traumatizing.

Many nights I have seen your face behind my closed eyelids, how you lie there at night so peacefully asleep, and how I lie next to you, admiring and full of love I

*look upon your sleeping face. As I come closer to you
very slowly and out of pure longing for your warm soft
skin, your warm breath and your sweet scent I gently
place my lips on your lips and enjoy your closeness
with all my heart.*

*Many times I have dreamed of this and also to hold you
in my arms, to be so very close to you and to feel your
heartbeat, to hear it; an organ which I am very grateful
to hear that it beats in my beloved's chest, so that my
heart – my dearest and sweet heart – is alive.*

*I am grateful to every fibre of your body from the
bottom of my heart, so that you enjoy good health and I
can also enjoy your life, BECAUSE you are alive!*

ON 18TH DECEMBER – AT NIGHT

*You're the mysteriously thing I've ever met. I only see
the good in you and repress the drama we both went
through. Although it fights inside of me that I have to
hate you so that my heart may be given a little
satisfaction after all the shame. I hate you and I love
you. Probably more loving than hating, but there is a
rough wind within me that advises me to hate you and
let you go.*

*Two hearts are beating in my chest; one, being black as
the deepest night and full of hate, and one, being bloody
red as glowing lava and full of love. Both of these hearts
beat with eagerness in my breast and want to be the
only true heart, which from now on should beat only as
the main heart. But both of these hearts are currently
my main hearts. Because both determine the moods that
tell me what I have to feel for you and with which fibre*

of my whole being I have to love you.
It confuses me and makes me fall into despair.
With what pure feeling can I confront you and tell you
here and now that I love you and that I mean it at all
times and not saying in a few days that I hate you, but
to mean it forever?
O thou nastiest bliss under the heavens, how innocent
thou art, and yet the evil that blinds my eyes drives thee
forth....
With how much painful bliss will heaven punish me,
never to forget you, never to be near you and never to
be able to give you a kiss?
As sweet as the bliss is, so painful its strokes ...

ON 19THE DECEMBER – IN THE MORNING

O my sweet heart! How long are you going to torture
me? How long will the fire consume my heart, burn it?
When will it be completely burned and decay to ashes?
O you sweet passion, not much longer and I burn,
when will you save me from the hot flames of despair?
Whose authority do you have to torment me like this
and to heat up my heart without being able to comfort
and love it thereupon?
How long do I have to torture myself to think of you, to
desire you, to love you and to want to feel your
heartbeat? Oh, heavens, how much longer? I'm dying
of longing! O lovely Sweety, save me!
What a sweet countenance! I admire your sweet facial
features, your sweet nose, your heavenly eyes, your
sweet mouth, your velvety soft skin. Your dark head of
hair shimmers so beautifully and softly and your divine

visage, which enchants me completely.
What mild and gentle language of the heart do I have to
apply in order to describe your essence in an ideal and
correct way? You are like an angel whose bliss and
heavenly appearance is impossible to describe. You are
like an angel whose wings are missing and yet who is
walking on this earth. Your heart is not flawless and
not pure, but pure and fine enough to please my heart.
Your heart is beautifully and brilliantly standing in
front of mine, and with all its devotion it knows
nothing more than to constantly admire your heart and
face. Thereupon, you wonderful and infinitely sweet
creature, you will have my admiration and devotion.

ON 19THE DECEMBER – IN THE EVENING

It's a sweet pain that accompanies me to miss you and
to love you hopelessly. It may hurt endlessly, but it is
lovely and sweet. Day and night I carry your sight in
my heart and yearn for your closeness, O you my
golden hope! Be my light and guide me the way, my
sweet star. May a thousand angels accompany and
protect you, and may your guardian angel care for you.
I'd love to be your angel, you cute little darling, being
very keen to be a part of you. But it's not what heaven
wants, unfortunately. My darling, my gold, my
heavenly light - please do not forget me, for I will not
forget you.
I can't sleep, I'm just thinking of you, you're robbing
me of my dreams, which I would have dreamed instead.
You make me want to die, because I can't stand this

empty feeling without you for long. Help me, my love! I'm drowning in you. You're my cosmos and the planets are all about you. You are what keeps me alive, my foothold, the sun, my breath; how could I live on without you, how can you require such a thing of me? I'm lost without you, how can I survive without you? You may think now, why is she so obsessed with me, why doesn't she just leave it to be good, why does she keep warming up old stories and can't forget them? My darling, I can't explain it, I don't know. It's not easy to get away from you, to forget you, believe me. We have experienced so much together, so many things hand in hand that my heart got used to being so close to you, despite the tragedy. You may easily forget me because you never loved me. For you, O sweet temptation, it seems the simplest thing in the world, but for me there has never been anything more difficult to overcome than this suffering, to have to carry your so sweet being forever in my heart.

Do not judge me, my sweet pain, methinks, my own heart has deceived me. It has turned away from me and henceforth lives its own life full of thoughts and love for you!

One should torment me alive in order to scream out and squeeze out these torments of the heart so that my heart, which has been tortured to death, can rest.

O you cute being, you sweet creature! Aren't you able to see how much I'm longing for you? Please don't allow that the flames of love burn me, perish me and kill me.

Be my salvation, sweet angel! Administer to me, have mercy, and deliver me from this punishment that is destroying me. Be my light and remember me.

Please, my heart, forgive my amorous being, forgive me for longing and agonizing over you. I know that you don't like it, that I long for you, love you and can never forget you, I know that it is unnerving you.... so, forgive me.

I need help and care, someone who keeps my heart, warms and loves it. O lovely sweet honey! My cute sparrow.... Forgive me that I am loving you...

ON 20TH DECEMBER – IN THE MORNING

Oh dearest! So many girls take a shine to you and make mooneyes at you. You don't defer to it, but in spite of that jealousness burns inside of me. All those girls are so close to you and I'm so far away. All those girls can always be close to you and wrap you around their finger at any time while I'm left many, many miles and hours away from you and try to make you beautiful eyes in vain.

O delightful gracefulness, how unjustly I am treated by this world, how deceived I feel by my own heart! Knowing – lonely sitting and with a fervent heart – that you are exposed to all these women, drives me into a deep raving madness. How sorry I have to feel myself suffering such an obsession with a human being!

No girl in the world is able to love you with as much heart and with as such ardent love as I would, O beloved! I am driven to insanity to know you amidst all these girls who are looking at you desirously and who,

like me, are also looking for your closeness as if there
were no other man on this earth.
But you can't blame them, because your sweet
countenance is attractive, that's true! And yet my heart
is furious because of all these wenches who are striving
for the death of my heart to get you. But I do not give
them this triumph.

'You shall not throw pearls before swine,' it says in the
Holy Scriptures. Thereupon, beloved, I will fight for
your favor. Many times I've fought for your heart and
many times I've had to avow myself beaten.
But this time I will fight until your heart glows with
love for me.
Even if it means death to me ...

On 20th December – At Noon

Then, my sweet beloved golden good, I will fight for you
as never before a wench has been able to fight for a
man's heart.
It is still a mystery to me, how I should controvert and
fight such a battle. But love can tell me and lead me to
victory, I am sure of that. There is no giving in, not
even when the Grim Reaper's eyes meet mine, but I
remain steadfast and willing to close you in my arms at
the end of the rocky, hard and bloody struggle and to
give you all the love through which I have almost
perished so many times and which tortured me so
endlessly. For you, my sweet beloved, I will endure this
battle, I will walk through the long paths of hell,
traverse dark paths of pain and defeat all the evil
demons on the way to you, to stand on the Victory

Mountain at the end and to look in the bright sunlight at your beloved sweet countenance. My spirit will triumph and rejoice and my mouth will praise and honor God, the Lord, that I may be together with and feel him — the beloved on this earth.

Oh my honey-sweet love, wait for me, count the hours in which I will be with you and receive your love, when I have won the victory.... for that amount of time, my heart, do not forget me, for otherwise the fight is lost. Crossed hell for nothing, defeated the demons for nothing.

Oh, please! I beseech you, my lovely sweet! Don't give up, just like I don't give up. I'll see you in the end. The struggle of love begins.

And may I perish in it, so be sure that until the last breath I asked only for your well-being, coveted your heart and only wanted to feel your warm breath. When my last breath will be done, words of love for you were on my lips, until the ice cold hands of death embraced me and carried me away into the other world.

My obituary for the world will be:

A girl with a heart full of love,
her truelove away from her,
cold death carried her away,
his stony heart as heavy as lashes....

* * *

Silence.

The just man stared at all the lines. Lines of a dead woman.

His heart threatened to burst with pain.

The letters fell out of his hands. He couldn't believe what was written there. The way she saw him, left him behind. Emptiness and severe nausea laid down on the just man. It was as if his love had died a second time.

The just man was neutral in gender. He loved this female creature — a lot. But it didn't seem like what she wanted. It was indescribable how this love was like. Like siblings, like friends? Yes. And yet more. Like lovers? Yes. And yet less. He doesn't know how to name this love, but it was strong, no matter what kind. And yet it seemed to have killed her ...

She thought, he never loved her. That's how she understood him. There was also never a reason for her to be jealous, for the just man had no interest in others. It was like that since her earliest youth and she knew about it.

He thought ...

The same applies to the voice she spoke about, which a heart better should have, in order to be able to interpret and follow its feelings more easily; the just man's heart knew there was such a voice. It possessed such a voice itself, the owner of which became incessantly audible. But most people don't hear the voice of their heart, they don't hear it and can't follow it.

What a soul fight his love had to endure because of him! What pain she had to suffer because of him!

O woe is me!

The just man buried his face in both hands. I killed her! A flood of tears flowed out of him, a huge wave forged ahead and flooded everything that could not withstand. A terribly red-hot lava crossed his heart, the hot sword raged wildly in his chest. The cry of hell was resounded in him, the little just heart was running on empty. Glowing coals scorched it, the blood boiled and steamed and made massive waves. A cruel roar filled the chest of the just man, the biting pain now gained the mastery. The darkness raised its regiment and led its terrible army across the little heart. It was wildly screaming and flailing around. His blood heated beyond measure. Torments of hell and terrible torture seized the little heart, his tears could not extinguish the biting flames. Pain was tormenting the heart heavily, his body was wounded severely. Serious distress superimposed onto this, bumping and with dropouts it continued to throb. The just man grasped horrified at his chest. His face showed bloodshot swollen eyes and many tears.

His heart stumbled many times, the just man remained sitting on the floor in shock. He waited until his heart had calmed down. Though he felt like dying ...

* * *

Slowly the little heart recovered, not completely, but so that it could beat more gently. The hellfire continued to burn in the just man's chest, his heart was exhausted, dead and tired.

It looked with empty and sad eyes, and wished it had never been born.

How is it to continue beating now?

How is it ever getting cheerful again?

Thus the days passed by — but heavy and drawn-out. The just man fought his way through the day. His housekeeper tried hard to cheer him up with hot love, after she found out what had happened. But he never touched the drink again. Day in, day out, he sat immovably in his wingchair in front of the fireplace and stared straight ahead with soulless, dead, expressionless and cried-empty eyes. How dead he was sitting there. Didn't move, didn't say anything, didn't eat anything. That's what also happened to the little heart in his chest. Like being dead inside it only beat monotonous, without joy and it only vegetated.

Wasn't it better if it just stopped dead?

Then it would be over.

For a long time it struggled with itself, remained alive only on the strength of goodwill. But one night it went too far for it. Resolutely — while the just man was asleep — it jumped out of his chest and immediately great unbridled joy and eagerness overcame it.

It wanted to know the world, other hearts, good things.

For a long time too much suffering and evil had laid over

the little heart, over its owner.

It wanted to get away.

Even if it had to act against the teachings of its master, who taught it never to deny the cup of sorrow and to remain steadfast, as being in a storm: someday this cup of sorrow will dry up, it cannot last forever. Just as a storm has a beginning, so it certainly has an end. But when did the end come in sight?

So the little heart had to flee, because otherwise it threatened to go out.

For a while the little heart looked upon the just man. His features were contrite as soon as his heart jumped out of his chest.

'I'm sorry, master,' whispered the little heart and gave him a little kiss on the deeply lined forehead. Then it hopped onto the window sill, opened the window and jumped out.

Freedom.

The little heart felt so lively, jaunty, weightlessly and independent as never before. The sword hanging across his chest was suddenly no longer there. Full of joy and without any pain, it just hopped away wherever it was going. Out into the world.

It was the middle of the night and pitch-black.

Everything laid in quiet peace to bed. At night peace laid over the lands of the earth, at night all weapons were silent. Oh, would it be always night and everyone would sleep!

But before wars are no longer existing, every human heart must change. The own wars, the quarrels with oneself and with others, one's own rejection and that of others, must stop and the inner wars before the outer ones come to an end.

Because when people's hearts change, all weapons automatically remain silent forever. For when people's hearts are filled with benevolence and love, there is no reason for enmity. That's how it will be.

When the children of men begin to recognize each other as brothers and sisters, it is only then that the globe will come to rest, and only then will terrorists, politicians, dictators and the rulers of each people will be able to calm down and, through their own inner peace, be able to eradicate the external war.

Unless this time, only the night will rule as peace before the day can, too.

A war will never succeed in creating peace.

Unless he extinguishes all humans.

Then there will always be silence on the globe when there is no one left.

When there is no longer loud life in the world, then only peace can work. Of course, the human race will ensure it. They work hard on it every day.

Refreshed, the little heart kept jumping without any aim. Everything laid empty in front of him, the whole world beamed at it. After some time, however, the little heart became so tired from jumping that it had to yawn constantly. So it quickly looked for a nice place where it could rest for a short time and move on soon afterwards. The place was soon found and the little heart—as soon as it fell down—slumbered away dainty and gently.

* * *

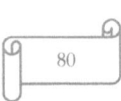

On the other hand, the way the little heart has been woken up was rude: It jounced and shook. And it fluctuated.

The little heart heard men's voices talking across each other. It sat up and looked around. Only now in the bright daylight was the little heart able to see something. But nothing it saw reminds it of something. None of them knew it. Where did it end up?

Suddenly something jumped out behind a box. It was a heart! However, it was slightly black, the red was very dark.

The little heart — being bright red — kindly smiled at the other heart. Society! It was rejoicing.

When the other heart noticed it, its eyes narrowed. 'Who are you? What are you doing here?' Its voice was hard and scratchy.

The little heart was scared. Why was it so rough? 'I... me,' it stammered, 'I don't know where I am. You've my apologies! I laid down to sleep in the middle of the dark night and now I'm awake and I don't know where I am.' The little heart seemed slightly desperate.

The other heart — having deep scars all over the body —
looked at it skeptically. 'Well, for all I care. You're a
stowaway. I don't care. But just stay calm, all right? If
they catch you, that's the last time you've pounded, all
right? If we land, you can disembark.'

The little heart didn't understand. 'Disembark? Where
are we here then?' Quizzically, it looked at the other
heart.

It looked at the little heart as if it wasn't all there. 'Is this
supposed to be a stupid joke? We're on a ship, boy!
Where have you lived? In a cave?' Laughing mockingly,
this rough heart disappeared in a hatch and left the little
heart alone.

What then is a ship?, asked the little heart and was
brooding over it. Could probably come close to a moving
house or a car — only bigger — where you can also live in
it.

The little heart produced the craziest ideas and sat there
and behaved calml,, as he was called.

Eventually, however, it was difficult to make out how

much time had passed — has it been hours or even days? — the little heart couldn't stand it any longer and jumped carefully — and anxious to remain unnoticed — on the deck of the ship.

Laughing and grunting men's voices were to be heard, and the little heart peeped out from behind a corner to see what kind of men they were.

It got sight of a horde of men — dressed all in black — having scars across the face, each wearing a full beard, and also each of them wearing a sword on their belts. What kind of men were they?

Then the little heart noticed hearts in the back of a corner on deck. They stood together, laughing and shouting as well. Some of them were dark red, others black as the night.

The little heart was scared. What did these colors mean? Weren't then all hearts bright red?

The pack did not seem to notice the little heart, everything here was so dark and venturously. So that the bright red colour of the little heart did not attract attention, it remained under cover. It felt itself in danger, something like this it had never felt before.

It wished itself off this ship. As soon as possible.

Or should it try to pull these people to its side, to get them to do better? Was that possible?

It was so deeply absorbed in his reflections that it did not even notice how the other hearts came towards it and ended up standing in front of it.

The little heart was scared.

The pitch-black heart — apparently the leader — stood right in front of the little heart and grinned diabolically.

'So what have we got here? A bright red heart with a fresh wound!' It laughed scratchy.

The little heart was wondering. Wound? It looked down, and indeed — a freshly scarred blood-red wound ran across its body! Produced by the hot sword. It wasn't there anymore, but it had left its mark.

Shocked, the little heart looked at the black heart. It seemed to be full of evil, its whole body was full of scars, crusts, bumps and calluses. The little heart tried to make out its master and looked over at the men. Immediately he recognized an equally wounded elderly man. Out of him spoke as much evil as from his heart.

'So,' rasped the evil heart, 'what do you want here? Damn you, you wayward bright red tomato!' Again a nasty laugh, in which the rest of the hearts – including the heart, which the little heart had already got to know before – agreed. 'Are you then a tomato?'

The little heart became sad. Why was everyone so mean to him? What was it doing wrong? Because it had the wrong color? Because it was different? Was that a reason?

'I'm here unintentionally,' the little heart started with a squeaky voice. 'I'll be out of here as soon as we dock.' Hopefully it looked at the other hearts. The black heart grinned ugly with his arms crossed in front of the chest at the little heart.

'I'll tell you how things are going now,' this one started. His voice was frightening. 'It will be a while before we dock. If we ever will. Sometimes we travel for years.'

The little heart did not know what the black heart was driving at.

It came closer and closer to the little heart. 'And you

know what? We don't want you here. You don't belong here. And we don't want to wait until we dock either. Do you understand?'

The little heart nodded. 'But... what can I do?' it desperately wanted to know.

'Oh,' the black heart laughed derisively. '**You** can't do anything' — the little heart breathed in panic — 'but **we** can do something,' the black heart went on croaking and snapped his fingers.

The little heart didn't quite understand.

Immediately, however, the hearts fell on the little heart and grabbed it tightly on its arms.

'Let go of me!' screamed the little heart. 'What are you up to?'

The black heart laughed diabolically. 'Oh, you're about to see that.'

The hearts yanked and pulled at the little heart, which now called fervently: 'Love one another'.

The black heart laughed. 'Eh, what? What's the point of that? You're talking stupid nonsense!' Diabolic loud

laughter was following. He looked at the little heart
amusedly. The others did the same as their leader. They
watched the desperate little heart with amusement.

'Put on then compassionate hearts, kindness, humility,
meekness, and patience, bearing with one another and, if one
has a complaint against another, forgiving each other.
And above all these put on love, which binds everything
together in perfect harmony. '

The little heart looked at the black heart mildly. In the
hope that it may wake up and become another. The black
heart, however, looked at the little heart angrily, it
sparkled out of its eyes in a rage.

It was like it was about to burst.

'Thank you,' it hissed through his clenched teeth, 'that
you showed us how little you belong to us. Love is for
cowards and little girls!'

The little heart didn't understand. 'But... why?'

'Throw it overboard!' the black heart roared without any
further explanation and while the little heart tried to
defend itself against it with its own strength, the black
heart only laughed out loud.

Then the evil hearts threw the just little heart overboard the ship and watched joyfully as it was swallowed by the sea.

Seven

When the just man woke up in the morning, he was unusually angry. And depressed and irritable.

He couldn't say why it was like that.

Was it the consequence of the emotional pain he had suffered?

'Damn it!' The just man complained what he had never done before in his whole life, not once, and he wondered — not to mention scared — not even about it.

Bitter-featured he got up and dressed.

When he came into the kitchen, the housekeeper stood there and prepared his breakfast. With a happy face she looked at the just man. 'A beautiful good morning, Sir,' she exclaimed. The just man stared at her coolly, did not reply.

The housekeeper did not let herself be deterred and continued her work.

'Will dinner be ready soon?' the just man moaned irritably.

'Coming up,' the housekeeper replied, attributing the ungracious tone of the just man to all the suffering he had to endure.

'Well, hopefully! And woe betide it's not tasty!' The just man watched the housekeeper unimpressed and cool while working in the kitchen. Shortly afterwards, she placed his breakfast in front of the just man and wished him good appetite.

The just man did not respond and began to eat.

'And does it taste good?' the housekeeper wanted to know friendly.

The just man looked at her with discontent. 'Not too bad. Could be better.'

The housekeeper now looked at the just man in horror. What had gotten into him? Was it really just the soul's sorrow that changed him so much? Did he realize that being good only causes torture and therefore he had shed it? No—that can,t be true. And he didn't even pray before dinner! He usually does that!

'What then are you staring at?' the just man snapped at the poor housekeeper, who turned away immediately.

'Excuse me,' she replied and ran out of the kitchen in a hurry.

* * *

"I'm going for a walk, woman,' the just man shouted to
his housekeeper and before she could say anything about
it, he was already out of the door.

What's wrong with him?

The housekeeper decided when the just man returned
home to prepare hot chocolate for him. Maybe it will lift
the spirits.

The just man stomped discontentedly and grim-featured
along the street, didn't greet back, knocked over where
he could and didn't recognize anyone to hold a natter
and to inquire about their wellbeing.

The people around him, who were accustomed to a
completely different treatment of him, stopped and
looked at each other confusedly and looked frowning
after the just man.

They all knew well about his suffering, but they also
knew that the just man was a fighter and always acted
rightfully. His morals wouldn't let anything upset his
goodness. He even embraced the cup of sorrow with

love — like a loved one — and lived through whatever life claimed from him with patience, faith and confidence. The just man has always been strong in his just nature and always knew how to solve every situation right. Could someone like that have been overthrown by suffering?

Of course, never before was the just man affected by something like this and hit him so hard, so that you could have made a comparison from the past.

People were surprised and left it at that for the time being. The just man surely was only a human being as well.

He was allowed this period of mourning with all the grief that was necessary. And one hoped for the return of the well-known just man.

He — in turn — was not aware of all this, he wanted to be left alone and not having to change his gaze or his words with anyone.

He walked around thinking about whether he eventually should go to a pub once in a while and order a beer.

He'd never done that before.

He hurriedly made his way to such a place and gained astonished glances when he entered.

'I want a beer,' the just man exclaimed and sat down at the bar.

'Yes, Sir. Immediately,' the landlord replied and hurried to fill the beer into a glass.

All the others were just staring at the just man who felt the staring eyes in his back. He cleared his throat. 'Do you know why everyone's staring so silly?' he asked the innkeeper, who now put the beer on his table.

Surprised by his flippant way of expressing himself — who otherwise knew him on the street with a different vocabulary — he hesitated a little before he replied: 'Well, you've never been here before and actually you've always renounced alcohol... haven't you?'

The just man nodded. 'Yes, that may certainly be true,' and took a long drink of his cool beer.

* * *

Hour after hour passed and the just man ordered more and more beer. He stayed until late in the evening, and drank and chatted with nice ladies who had always admired him so highly.

He was getting more and more drunk and boisterous. Many people wondered what had become of this otherwise so good and just man and watched his exuberance critically and disapprovingly.

'Life is to good to spend it in a mood of dejection and in keeping with rules and commandments!' the just man exclaimed, grabbing one of the ladies who simply loved to marry him and gave her a passionate kiss. She was so overwhelmed that she wrapped her arms around him and completely abandoned to him.

The innkeeper shook his head uncomprehendingly.

After all — it was almost midnight — the just man returned home. In other words, the lady who had been kissed by him helped him home and found the worried housekeeper, who had been waiting for him with hot chocolate all day long.

'But what the heck has happened?' shouted the

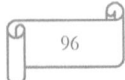

housekeeper in shock.

'He's got tight all day,' the lady explained, 'and all the ladies have been smothered with kisses by him.'

The housekeeper breathed in alarmed. 'Say what?'

The lady nodded. 'Yes, that's right. I don't understand it, too. Even his cruel manner. He's so different.'

Together, the housekeeper and the lady tried to heave the just man into the large wingchair in the library. The hot chocolate was cold.

'Thank you for bringing him home,' said the housekeeper.

The lady nodded. 'You are welcome.'

What had changed the just man so much? So totally turned upside down? What was going on?

The housekeeper decided to stay with him for the time being and spend the night there to stand by the just man if anything happens.

In his wingchair he had immediately disappeared in deep alcoholic sleep, so that the housekeeper prepared a bed for the night in a room upstairs.

What a broken heart and the loss of loved ones can cause,

the housekeeper thought, when she was lying in her bed.
Pain can make a person very malevolent. It can numb
you so badly that you don't even know what you're
doing or saying. Or you don't care. That everything is
perceived as if through a veil. Unreal. Not here. So it
doesn't matter.

The just man had never sought alcohol before. So that
would mean it was something serious this time.

This caused great concern to the housekeeper. How was
she able to help the just man?

Of course she wanted to give him his time of mourning
and give him time to regain his composure. But this
could take an eternity. Should the just man remain a
mean, stunned, unseemly, dishonorable man for so long?
The housekeeper couldn't let that happen.

Considering that, she appreciated him too much.
Afterwards, she would blame herself if the just man was
the old self again and had done all kinds of mean things
until then, that she had not saved him, since she was
clearly in her head.

Icy coldness.

Soaking wet.

Stranded on a shore, all alone and saddened.

The just heart had struggled with great effort through the icy cold seawater, swallowed water here and there, had breathlessness and had almost fallen victim to blindness. For hours it had been drifting in the sea, struggling for hours for its life. It wasn't until midnight that it was unconsciously driven ashore, where it eventually regained consciousness. Now shivering it wandered about in an unknown city, and saw nothing in the darkness. A street light shone here and there to be sure, but the just heart could not perceive much.

Only, that it was strange here.

What kind of place was it?

As it continued to bounce along the street, it heard voices shouting across each other. And then it identified light shining out of one of the windows onto the dark street, and its glow laid on it like a luminous cover.

The just heart was curious and jumped to this glowing window to peek in. When it looked inside, it opened its eyes wide open with surprise.

To the innocent little heart it seemed Sodom and Gomorrha were ruling there, but it continued to watch spellbound as people sat at several tables, who were repeatedly served drinks and food by nice ladies and everyone caterwauled and roared. What happened here? It was abhorrent to the just heart to enter through the front door, alone, since it was apparently the only awake house, and it was perhaps blissful there, in spite of the fact that there was poaching going on, so that it looked for another entrance to slip in. Maybe it would once again encounter a company of hearts!

But a nice one ...

So the just heart tried to get into this house and finally found an open window. Quickly it jumped in and — as soon as it entered the house — found a soft and comfortable blanket, which it put it round its little body and laid down comfortably with it.

'I'd be careful, if I were you, little shaver,' the just heart heard it suddenly coming out of the dark corner.

It was the voice of an old heart.

'Who are you?' asked the just heart.

The old heart laughed, but did not yet emerge from the darkness and could hardly recover. Severe coughing attacks accompanied the laughter.

'What's wrong with you?' the just heart wanted to know.

'Oh,' the old heart began, 'a little shaver like you breaks in here and asks a long-time resident man who you are,' it followed another laugh. The just heart was terrified. Broke in?

'No, I didn't break in. So, not in the classical sense,' the just heart replied ashamed.

Now the old heart stepped out of the darkness and one recognized that it wore a white beard and many wounds on the body.

The just heart knew nothing to say.

'I've been living here for almost a hundred years, boy,' it started croaking, 'my master' — it turned to the darkness — 'is dying there. It's only a matter of time before I come to an end. When I have no power anymore to keep pumping blood.' The old heart looked hopefully, despite these sad words.

But the just heart was terrified. 'You must die?' Distorted with pain, it looked at the old heart. This nodded mildly smiling.

The just heart looked sad to the ground. The old heart came nearer, put his arm around it and said: 'Behold, my boy, this is the world: one comes to go. But if you have lived a good life, done good deeds, if you have loved honestly and a lot, then the end is not terrifying. It's redemption.'

The just heart looked to the old heart at the last word. His master once said this, too. The word seemed familiar to him.

'Nothing in this world is eternal, everything leaves someday. This includes summer, winter, rain and snow. It comes, it goes, it returns at some point, it returns home. Tell me, how young is your master?'

The old heart looked at the just heart mildly. 'Way out of his childhood,' it replied. The old heart was wide-eyed. 'And yet you are so young and in sound condition?'

The old heart couldn't believe it.

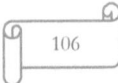

'Your master must be a very good, wise and young-stayed decent man who knows how to live life well.'

The just heart nodded. 'That's him. Certainly.'

The old heart smiled kindly. 'This is a real treasure. But what's happened? Why are you here? You can't live here in the rotten!'

The just heart nodded. 'That's right. I'm from somewhere else. I ran away.'

The old heart now looked at him questioningly.

'With a gentleman like you've got? Why the heck?'

The just heart did not know how to answer. 'I could not endure the pain that befell my master. It hurt too much. I have disregarded his teachings to drink the cup of sorrow empty until the last sip, and have gone away.' It looked down depressed.

The old heart smiled with understanding.

'I can understand that. The world is a real battlefield. After all, you — as the heart — are the one who has to fight these battles. But no matter how painful life comes in, always remain true to yourself, to your virtues, your good words and works. Never let life change you to the negative, that you fall and surrender, and that you for the sake of convenience forget and discard everything that is good and what is worth fighting for. Your master is now without heart, and so respected and good as he may have been before, now he is cold and hard without you and made of stone.' The just heart was terrified.

The old heart continued: 'You will not find a single place in this world without pain and suffering. Not a single one. Even if you flee so far, a life without suffering cannot succeed.'

The old heart smiled at the just heart. This, however, did not understand. 'Why? Why can't there be a life without suffering? What's the point?'

Whoever takes part in a competition will only receive Victory's Laurels if he fights according to the rules. So remain faithful in all your deeds, and strive diligently in my vineyard; God Himself will be your reward. Eternal life is truly worth all these and even more difficult fights. Then you will no longer have to complain, for death will lose its power, my son, think of the fruits of this hardship, of its imminent end and of the overabundant reward, so you will not feel all this as a burden,

but as a source of 'greatest consolation' in your life of patient

endurance. Hold out when you're being chastised. God treats

you like sons and daughters. For where is a son, a daughter,

whose father does not chastise them? For whoever has suffered

in the flesh has ceased from sin.'

Suffering cleanses the soul, burns out evil when viewed

as a means of salvation and not as a punishment. Life is a

short period of time, but eternity is eternal. You choose

what life you want to live for.'

The old heart had finished his wise speech and now

looked at the just heart knowingly. 'I understand ... .'

It became thoughtful. 'But there are also souls who have

suffered much and are evil all the same.'

The old heart nodded. 'Yes, there are. This happens

because there is no faith as a solid rock against which the

long-suffering storm can bluster. If your house is built on

sand, the floods will tear it away. And if one does not

know about the preciousness of suffering — of the

crosses — one sees this as a punishment. Feels betrayed by

the world, left in the lurch. Firm souls anchored in faith

stand steadfastly in the storm, because they know why all this. That they expect a reward.'

The just heart looked up in astonishment. 'How do you know all this?'

The old heart laughed silently. 'Because my master is such a soul. He will hopefully be rewarded for having fought so hard through many crosses throughout his long life, my boy.' A mild smile underlined this statement, which impressed the just heart. 'Once he has died, his suffering maltreated soul goes into the hereafter, into eternity. Up to heaven.'

'Amen,' whispered the just heart.

Suddenly the old heart paused, struggling for air. The just heart panicked. 'I will go away,' whispered the old heart distorted with pain and leaped back to his master, now lighting a candle.

The just heart followed him. The old heart sank into the chest of the old man — his master — and after a few last breaths, both of them laid there cold, still and breathless. Eternity.

'Farewell,' said the just heart. 'Farewell. In heaven. I hope we meet again. Someday.'

The days passed without any recovery in the nature of the just man.

He remained ice-cold and mean.

He turned away homeless persons gruffly.

He callously insulted people seeking advice or help and slammed the door shut in front of them.

The just man cursed, insulted, lied day in and day out and was not even aware of it.

His housekeeper was totally desperate about it. She had set herself out to prevent his wickedness against others. On the contrary, it was not so easy. He was just as vicious against her! He had obviously set himself the goal of insulting her every day and bringing her close to madness.

She suffered proper anxiety states in his company, so she was always happy when he got more and more often drunk in the inn.

Meanwhile, people were as well afraid of the just man and avoided him as best they could on the street. His face was filled with hatred.

No more smiles. No more exhilarating words.

No more scrips of paper with words of wisdom and consolation.

No more goodness, no more mercy, no more love.

The just man's enviers now laughed at this change that had already been foreseen, because when the just man then housed the poor man at his home and the patrons only had words of praise for him, the envious ones knew that this was not forever. One day, something would hit the just man who threw him off the track. That hit him so sharply in the middle of his heart that his goodness would have gone.

There were storms which — when they raged brutally — could also bring stones to their knees. One couldn't be steadfast forever, there was no such thing. On your own. Now that the just man seemed to be one of them, they seeked his company, cursing, drinking and chatting cheerfully together. So one late evening they gad about together, laughing and shouting and telling each other all sorts of dishonourable things.

Every now and then they came upon people who were still on the road late, shouting mean things or even throwing stones after them.

Suddenly they noticed a homeless person who had been sleeping on a bench and slept happily.

Laughing spitefully they stepped up to him. With a mischievous laugh they started to pester him, to pull him by the hair, to take his things away from him. The homeless man woke up frightened and recognized the just man who had often helped him with money, clothes and food. He looked at him happily, unaware of the changed nature of the just man. The homeless man recognized the diabolical grin in the just man's face and was frightened. What was going on here?

'Hey black man,' one of the other men started, 'what are you lying here? Get lost!' An ugly laugh followed.

The homeless guy panicked. 'I have nowhere to go. I don't own anything.'

The group laughed.

'So you're superfluous?' laughed one of the men loudly.

The homeless guy swallowed hard.

'Shall we free this city, this society from this superfluous riffraff?' the just man now mocked as well.

The homeless man got scared. Wide-eyed he stared at the just man. 'What's that supposed to mean?'

One of the men gave a spiteful laugh. Before the homeless man could see anything in the darkness — only by the sparse light of the streetlamp and the moon — one of the men brutally beat him down.

Being unconscious and bleeding he laid on the cold hard ground and the men kicked this homeless man until he was lying in a pool of blood. The just man, however, kept himself in the background. Yelling and laughing, they kept going on and on. Until they got bored, because the homeless man didn't show any more emotion.

Suddenly a sentence leapt in the just man's mind that he had once read: *Love does not rejoice at wrongdoing, but rejoices with the truth.*

He stood there for a moment and pondered about it.

He looked at the man lying on the floor, bleeding, appearing dead and... felt nothing.

* * *

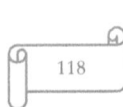

The news spread quickly in the city that someone had killed a homeless person in the night for no reason.

They hated me without a cause.

The perpetrators are on the run.

They were looking for witnesses. There have not been any so far.

The housekeeper heard this message and suspected something bad. Because the next day — after the just man returned home after a long night in the tavern — she recognized traces of blood on his shoes.

At first she believed he had hurt himself or something like that. But after this news, she now believed that the just man had something to do with this deed.

She blamed herself for not having saved him from this terrible act! But how? After all, she was at an advanced age and was in bed at night. Following the just man all the time like a little boy seemed to too much her, especially was this exceeding her powers.

This message about the manslaughter of a poor homeless person seemed to leave the just man cold.

There was no movement in him.

There were many who suggested this to the just man theoretically, but there was hardly anyone who seriously believed that he was actually capable of such a thing. So no one suspected him and he was left alone. The just man gradually began to displease his books in the library. They all dealt only with goodness, love for one another, brother and sisterhood! What's he going to do with odds and ends like that?

So he instructed his housekeeper to take all his books somewhere to burn or throw them away. Although she did this and took the books away, she secretly donated them to welfare. One didn't burn books, nor throw them away. So she gave them away for good. Now the just man stood in a library without books and with empty shelves. He grinned diabolically. 'I like that.'

The housekeeper shook her head without understanding and with a sorrowful heart.

Where is this going to lead?

* * *

Day in, day out, the just man disappeared outdoors most of the day. He usually got drunk in the pub. But it often happened that he had to let go of his anger at other people and frightened, saddened or provoked them with badly insulting remarks.

People slowly began to fear the just man. This was no longer a period of mourning — no. It seemed more as if the just man had ceased to be good, to believe in goodness. To believe in anything at all. As if the storm of life had pressed him down, defeated him.

The rock in the surf had sunk.

If it can knock down someone like him, people thought, what will happen to us when the storm comes?

All things are possible for one who believes.

So the darkness laid down over the city in which the just man lived, because now it no longer had got a good man to whom one could go if one needed advice, sought help, cast one's cares and desired warmth. Evil sought permanent entry into the just man's chest to form a hard, cold stone out of his hole — which the just heart had left behind — which he wanted to put in his chest, so that the good could never again rule over the just man.

Corruption, death and bitterness should follow him all

his life.

For days, the just heart pondered what the old heart had said. That its master was now icy cold and evil because of him, as it took the good morals, the virtues with him and its master had now fallen prey to immorality. Was that true?

Could this have destroyed his master now? Was he evil now? — Of course, he hasn't got a heart anymore.

It was known how people who were heartless behaved. Should it return home now, just now as it really started with this adventure journey? What had to be done?

For a long time the just heart pondered, indecisive about how to proceed.

The just heart roamed the streets of the new city and it could not think of an answer. It was too torn between.

His master would have wanted it to return, for the good, to remember what really counted. That it should do the right thing — even had to. No matter what price has to be paid for it.

Suddenly the just heart noticed another heart on its way. It was deep red. A few holes adorned his body, encrusted blood hung on it. Red, swollen eyes and a sad expression — so the just heart recognized — were also on this heart. The just heart approached this with full compassion.

'What's eating you, little heart?' the just heart wanted to know. The sad maltreated heart — it was female — looked terrified at the just heart.

'Please love me' it whispered desperately. 'Please.'

The just heart was touched by this desperate call for love.

'I'm dying of thirst' it continued quietly. 'Look at me.'

The just heart saw it. This heart stood in front of it dried-out and crusty.

'I love you, my daughter,' said the just heart full of mercy and opened his arms for a hug.

The sad little heart watched wide-eyed the unbelievable act of pure love of this heart for which it thirsted and jumped with longing into the open arms of the just heart. Immediately a great ocean of tears broke out from this and the just heart stroked over its head with whispering gentle, loving words.

'Calm, my little one,' whispered the just heart. 'I will give you as much love as you need. I'm here, daughter.

My love will flow through you, soak you, fill you up,
even drown you.'

The sad heart could hardly stop crying. The just heart
took its own sweet time for this poor, thirsty little heart
and comforted it. Everlasting they stood there on the
way, passing hearts pointed hatefully and diabolically
laughing at them, but the just heart was not deterred.

Do not judge by appearances, but judge with right judgment!
If you want to be good, to do good, it means many
sacrifices. And why justifying yourself — even be
ashamed — in front of heart-cold living beings because of
a loving act?

With all openness the just heart gave love, with all
goodness it gave comfort and friendship.

Was the world already at a point where it liked to spread
hatred publicly, but was ashamed of love in public?

O faithless and twisted generation, how long am I to be with
you? How long am I to bear with you?

Slowly the sad heart came to rest. The just heart looked at
it mildly. With both hands it gently covered its face.

From red, wet and desperate eyes it looked into the just,

knowing and gentle eyes of the just heart.

'Daughter,' started the just heart, 'tell me about your pain. What happened to you? Why don't they give you love?'

The sad heart swallowed further tears. 'This world is a place of ice-cold darkness,' complained it. 'Finding love – real, true, pure love – is like capturing a cloud. It's sheer impossible. The darkness, the cold and the malice – a dreadful pair of triplets – are ruling this place. With great success. If love still exists, it is usually only love of hate – unjust, dishonest, insidious love. You, my brother, seem to possess a rare gift. Being able to truly love without guile.'

The little heart looked at the just heart with small sad eyes.

Great compassion laid down on the just heart. 'You mean you were looking for true pure love, but found only insidious love, and so your wounds were made?'

The sad heart nodded. 'So it is. I loved so much. Very, very much. With my whole body. With every fibre; every beat I did was due to that other heart. But nothing came back. Just kicks, punches, stitches. I began to die of thirst. My blood supply was dwindling.'

The just heart could no longer hold back with emotion. It started to cry bitterly.

The sad heart watched him. But immediately tears came into its eyes again and it threw itself back into the arms of the just heart.

So now they stood embraced and bitterly weeping on the way and cried over this heart-cold world.

For a long time they stood there and endured the scorn and derision of passing hearts.

Then the just heart released the warm hug and looked into the empty, tear-dimmed, sad eyes of the little heart. It smiled at it gently. 'My daughter,' the just heart began, 'I know your body is destroyed, sorrow is sowed, pain is reaped. But if you fight, just for yourself, you will win. Never let others rule you, let others tell you how you have to be, what you have to feel, how you have to behave in a certain moment. How you should feel. It's all in your own hands. You alone can cause that everything one commanded, one does and one says to you, will not affect you. No living soul on earth has so much power to be someone else's ruler. Everyone is part of the whole, but no one stands above everything. Be aware of that. Love is the goal, and if only hate confronts you, pity these poor hearts. Hate often comes from pain. All those who hate have often experienced pain themselves. But everyone comes to term with it differently. Some remain strong and faithful to themselves and continue to be good; others abandon what is good and transform themselves into the very ones who have inflicted this pain on them.'

The just heart looked upon the sad heart with tenderness. It looked out of its little eyes in amazement and sniffed. 'Is that true?'

The just heart nodded gently smiling. 'Oh, yes. It is.'

For a while, the sad heart looked around thoughtfully.

'And,' the just heart restarted, 'beyond that, suffering has a deeper meaning. It causes cleaning. It makes one's own self good. Holy. Free from vices. If you allow this purification, you will win life. Only a few are aware of that.'

It smiled.

The sad heart got wide eyes. 'Is that true? How do you know that?'

The just heart smiled. 'That's what my master taught me. This are the rules of life.'

The sad heart was now completely fascinated. 'Who's your master, brother?'

The just heart breathed deeply. 'He is a just man, full of love and mercy. He plays the rules very well. His roots are deeply rooted in the earth of faith. No matter what things happen to him, love makes him to act right. He does not exercise violence — neither spiritually nor physically — he builds on justice, brings about peace, he teaches and keeps the right law, exercises neither retribution nor resistance, he loves his enemies, gives without demanding, forgives as many times as he can without bearing somebody any ill will, he does not judge anyone, because he himself is not without vice, and he builds fearless on God without asking, without doubting.' The just heart smiled at the sad heart that looked upon it with admiration. 'How does he do it?' breathed the sad heart.

The just heart shrugged its shoulders. 'I suppose he's not heartless and tries to understand and unite them all.'

The sad heart swallowed. 'But... you're here without him.'

The just heart did not understand at first, but then it understood too well. Shocked, it looked at the sad heart and nodded. 'Yes. That's true.'

Silence.

The sad heart now looked pityingly upon the just heart. 'Why did you leave him?' It was almost a whisper. The just heart looked at it desperately. 'His pain hurt me too much and so I left him cowardly. But I had no idea that the world is far more painful than his pain could ever be. That the hearts of this world are far worse than any evil that can strike you in your own house. I had no idea...'

'What do you intend to do now, my brother?' said the sad heart.

Walk while you have the light, lest darkness overtake you. The one who walks in the darkness does not know where he is going.While you have the light, believe in the light, that you may become sons of light,' said the just heart and the sad heart did not understand what it was supposed to mean, so that it waited for the just heart to say more.

'I will seek my master and save him from great vices, if that is still possible.'

The sad heart nodded. 'Yes. Yes. Good.'

Now it understood.

The just heart sighed heavily.

'What's wrong? Aren't you well?' the sad heart seemed worried.

'O daughter, if you only knew!' The just heart cried out desperately and fell to his knees sobbing on the cobblestones. The tears came down in streams and covered the ground.

The sad heart fell to the ground beside him. 'Well, brother, speak out.' The just heart looked up and in tears it shook its head. 'It's too bad.'

'No, my brother. Speak, no matter what it is. Let it out, let go.'

The just heart sniffed. It took a little while to calm down. 'My master, he was such a good man... so incomparable ... love in person.' It snivelled again.

'He was?' The sad heart was confused.

The just heart looked at it. It nodded. 'Yes. He was. Do think: When I—his heart—am gone, he is no longer good. He's heartless, cold, evil.'

Another sniffle.

The sad heart kept looking at it. 'But... you cannot know that...'

The just heart was shaking. 'Oh, yes, that's inevitable. How else could he be without a heart? He's like all the other people out there whose hearts are wandering alone. Why do you think they walk around alone? If they were in the chests of their masters, there would be no heartless people. Hence the word. Oh God!' Desperately it threw itself on the hard, cold ground. 'I had no idea!'

The just heart cried desperately. Hot tears broke out of it, old crusty wounds burst open and hot ruby-red blood flowed onto the cobblestones. The sad heart watched this dramatic scene with dismay. 'O brother! What's the matter with you?' the sad heart cried in panic, unable to do anything. What could it have done?

In pure despair and panic, the just heart began to dry up of both blood and tears.

The sad heart had to watch this as it bled to death on the open road in agony over this cold world, whose ruler was evil.

'My brother, when you're dying now, your master will never be good again, but dies with you and this in evil!' the sad heart cried out to the just heart. Immediately it was terrified by itself and paused in its despair.

'Make it well again, and you will do justly,' so strongly spoke the sad heart. The just heart looked up to this one and was amazed at these words.

'Dry your tears and then act.' The sad heart winked at him. The just heart sniffed, struggled clumsily to its feet with the help of the sad heart and nodded. 'Yes, you're right, daughter. Despair is useless. I must act. Standing up for my mistakes. Be strong.'

The sad heart smiled and nodded.

'That's right. And so am I. For my mistress I must go back and be strong. Strengthen her and equip her with faith.'

After the just heart and the sad heart had said goodbye to each other, each of them went their own way to live on and be strong for their individual human beings.

The just heart, however, had no idea where it was and how to find its way home. At that moment it longed so much for its master's chest to return home that it felt a biting sting. It dragged itself further along the road. Its body became heavier and heavier. The longing became so great that it could only pump on with difficulty.

Homesick.

Why oh why was existence a single cup of sorrow?

Was the earth-world in reality already hell? Damnation?

The heart was terrified. Why did it have such thoughts?

It already had the answer to existence. To suffering. Pain.

Death.

After all, the just heart had to lean against a wall to rest briefly. It closed its eyes. It needed a break, rest, recovery. There was just pure exhaustion.

The just heart breathed heavily. What was happening now all at once?

But then it suddenly felt something hot running down and it was frightened when it saw the blood running out of the encrusted wounds again.

The just heart sat on the ground. How could it prevent bleeding to death? How could it plug the wound? Panically it thought about, but nothing wanted to come into mind. It felt the cold and unconsciousness slowly seized hold of it. Heavy cold darkness overcame the just heart. Numbness of the limbs, dizziness and suddenly ... it stood still.

There were a small cool breeze and faded voices. Darkness. The unconsciousness exchanged its guard post with the consciousness. A pinpoint of light appeared. Floating.

What had happened?

A gentle voice to the left. A gentle, cool hand on the forehead. 'Wake up,' whispered the voice. 'Wake up.' Wake up? From what? Was this even a dream to wake up?

'Wake up.'

Consciousness pushed its way harshly into the foreground. It pulled its hand forward and forced its eyes to open. The just heart opened its eyes with a heavy loud gasp of relief. The point of light was further afield, the cool hand on the forehead belonged to a young heartlady who smiled kindly at the just heart.

'You're awake,' she whispered softly.

The just heart looked confused. 'What's happening? Where am I?'

The young heartlady kept smiling gently. 'You've stopped working. We have found you and revived you through massage. You must have been very exhausted. You've slept about three days.' She gently stroked its hand. The just heart swallowed. 'Three days? And... who's 'we'?'

The heartlady winked. 'The cardiac clinic. We are hearts of doctors and we know how to fix broken hearts again.'

At that moment an elderly heart with slightly gray hair entered, saw the just heart and exclaimed: 'Ah, he's awake.'

Happily he came to the bed of the just heart and gave it his hand. 'I am the chief and the attending physician here. I hope you recovered well? It was quite difficult to restart you.' He winked at the just heart. This one nodded. 'Yes. Thank you. I feel better.'

The doctor's heart smiled. 'Excellent.'

'I was on my way home and suddenly ...,' the just heart was searching for words. The doctor nodded knowingly. 'I understand.' Seriously, he looked at the just heart. 'Where's your home, if you don't mind my asking?'

The just heart shook its head desperately. 'I don't know. I was travelling. Without my master. I don't know where I am and how to get home.'

The heartlady and the doctor's heart looked at each other with compassion. 'My friend,' the doctor began, 'maybe

you can tell us what it looks like in your hometown. I get around a lot and maybe I can help you find your home.'
The just heart thought about. Could it tell anything? Does it know enough of the place where it lived? What it looked like. Didn't every place look the same?
'Well,' it started, 'I don't rightly know. There were ships, and I travelled on them.' It didn't really know to what extent this could be helpful to the doctor. He laughed. 'Oh, that's how it is! Well, I only know one place where there's a port nearby. Maybe this one is your home.'

'So all I have to do is walk straight ahead and I'm already at the local port, which will take me to the harbour of my homeland?' said the just heart.

The doctor's heart nodded. 'Yes, usually if all goes well. Of course, it always depends on where the ship is going. But your port and ours are the only ports that move back and forth with their merchant ships. I wish you well, brother.'

So the heartlady and the doctor's heart said good bye to the just heart.

This one did as it was called and only walked straight ahead to get to the harbour. After an endless walk, the just heart finally reached the harbour. But it saw not one single ship!

So it set itself on a stone and waited.

For a long time it was sitting there and wondering whether a ship ever would dock. It could count its blessings that his master had taught it the virtue of patience, and so the just heart waited with joyfulness. The cardiac clinic had done him pretty good. A few days of rest was something that was urgently needed and a real rarity in the world.

Now — early in the morning — it felt so refreshed that it continued its journey. But in the meantime the early morning turned into a radiant noon. The just heart looked around and suddenly saw a ship approaching at the far back! The just heart smiled. Finally!

However, it took a few minutes until the ship docked, so the just heart continued to wait.

When it finally landed and people came off the ship with large wooden crates in their hands, the just heart quickly jumped on board ship and hid in a corner. However, it did not want to stay on deck, it could be discovered. So it sneaked down unseen in a hurry and froze when it saw hearts sitting next to each other who caught sight of the just heart with a start.

'Who are you?' asked a middle-aged, wine-red heartlady and stepped towards the just heart. 'Do you want to rob us? These treasures' — she pointed to a corner where there were loads of jewels in a crate — 'belong to us.' She sounded hostilely.

The just heart smiled mildly.

'Which treasures? *Provide yourselves with moneybags that do not grow old, with a treasure in the heavens that does not fail, where no thief approaches and no moth destroys. For where your treasure is, there will your heart be also,'* so the just heart spoke and the hearts around it looked at each other in confusion.

'How is that supposed to mean?' a little heart wanted to know.

Take care, and be on your guard against all covetousness, for one's life does not consist in the abundance of his possessions. Therefore I tell you, do not be anxious about your life. Fear not, little flock!' The little heart smiled friendly.

It looked into the confused faces of the other hearts and waited.

'You speak like a sage,' whispered the heartlady in front of him. 'Is it you?'

The just heart kept smiling. It looked directly at the lady and said: 'I would not call myself wise, because I have been taught everything I know by my master, who is certainly wise.'

'And why do you say something against our fortune?'
the lady wanted to know more.

'If one gives it to the poor, it doesn't matter,' the just
heart spoke. 'But: *This night your soul is required of you, and
the things you have prepared, whose will they be?* ' it
continued speaking.

The lady looked at the just heart in shock. So it kept
going: *'So is the one who lays up treasure for himself and is
not rich toward God. And which of you by being anxious can
add a single hour to his span of life?* '

The just heart looked mildly around one.

Nobody said anything.

'He's right,' then the little heart called. 'He's right.'

The other hearts looked at the little heart flabbergasted.

'Excuse me?'

'Yes, do think: we are hearts! If we don't behave well,
who's going to do it? As we are, we allow our masters to
be the same! It's not just us! It affects others. We'll die
sometime and rot. But the Spirit—He will go there, just
after his heart. It was good, it was bad... Where do you

go? Everything depends on it,' continued the little one.

The just heart was highly refreshed to hear something so true from another heart and smiled heartily.

'Amen!' The just heart winked at the little heart and this one giggled sweetly. It was obviously a child's heart.

Then the just heart cleared its throat and said: 'Why I am here: I'm on my way home. To my master.'

'Where is that?' the child's heart exclaimed immediately.

'I'm afraid I have no idea,' said the just heart. 'I don't know what this place is called. All I know is that there's a port, too.'

The elderly heartlady looked at him apologizing. 'Well, since we've been on the way for days, and also for now when we cast off from here, we won't be able to land so quickly, I don't know whether we can get past your place or even let you out of there, even if we knew it exactly.'

The just heart looked worried.

'But we must help him!' called the child's heart and jumped up. 'Somehow.'

The heartlady disregarded it. 'We're very sorry.'

'No!' screamed the child's heart.

The just heart gently placed a hand on the head of the child. 'Don't worry about it. I'll find a way.'

It smiled mildly.

The heartlady looked upon the just heart coolly and condescendingly. 'So can I assume you'll leave our treasure alone?'

The just heart looked at her. *For you are not setting your mind on the things of God, but on the things of man. You received without paying; give without pay. Acquire no gold or silver or copper for your belts. Enter by the narrow gate. For the gate is wide and the way is easy that leads to destruction, and those who enter by it are many. For the gate is narrow and the way is hard that leads to life, and those who find it are few.'*

It looked gently at the heartlady, who now swallowed hard.

Everyone was looking at him with reverence. Then the heartlady cleared her throat and said even cooler: 'I wish you would leave, you are not welcome here. Your convictions are out of place here. Besides, we don't see any way to help you.' Ice-eyed she looked at the just heart.

This one looked at the heartlady with mild eyes and spoke: *'And as you wish that others would do to you, do so to them. Neither do I condemn you. You judge according to the flesh; I judge no one. Yet I do not seek my own glory; there is One who seeks it, and he is the judge.'*

The just heart looked upon the heartlady with love. She swallowed hard again and shrugged her shoulders.

'Well, if you say so. There, sit with us!'

The children's heart squeaked with joy and the just heart smiled with tears of joy in its eyes.

He stepped up to the others and sat down with them.

But the heartlady snorted scornfully and stepped to her treasure. Her eyes were riveted by it with admiration.

The just heart received great compassion for her, because her whole being was completely engrossed in earthly burdens. She was not free, therefore her dissatisfaction and coolness.

'A person cannot receive even one thing unless it is given him from heaven,' the just heart spoke softly into the room, but no one understood what it meant. So it continued: *'It is*

the Spirit who gives life; the flesh is no help at all.'

The heartlady heard what it said, but did not turn to him and ignored it. But shortly afterwards it broke out of her: 'If you have anything against wealth, at least leave those alone who have it and stay away from it.' She was almost screaming.

Everyone flinched upset, but the just heart sat resolutely, fearlessly and gently smiling there. 'As I said before, if you give it to the poor, it doesn't matter. My master is also rich, but gives much of it to those who have nothing. I have something much more powerful, more beautiful and richer than wealth itself,' said this mildly.

The heartlady laughed spitefully. 'Oh, yeah? And what? Wisdom?'

The just heart smiled. 'No. A good, free existence. Virtues, a clear conscience. God.'

The heartlady laughed diabolically. 'Aha!'

The just heart kept speaking: *You who were once slaves of sin have become obedient from the heart to the standard of teaching to which you were committed, and, having been set free from sin, have become slaves of righteousness.'*

The heartlady now looked thoughtfully.

'Free yourself, my daughter,' said the just heart, 'have courage.'

All through our lives we meet anger, jealousy, and trouble.

Things disturb us; we live with furious conflicts and with the

fear of death. Even when we go to bed, we think up new

troubles in our sleep.

We get little rest, if any at all. When we sleep, it is as if we

were awake, disturbed by our imaginations. If we dream that

we are running from an enemy, just as we are about to be

caught, we wake up and are relieved to find there is nothing to

be afraid of.

These are what all creatures, both human and animal, must

face (but it is seven times worse for sinners): death, violence,

conflict, murder, disaster, famine, sickness, epidemic. All these

things were created because of the wicked; they are the ones

who have caused destruction. Everything that comes from the

earth goes back to the earth, just as all water flows into the sea.

The just man woke with a start.

He was bathed in sweat. His pulse was racing.

It was midnight.

Those words... a memory flashed.

Wherefrom did he know it? What was the meaning?

The memory of goodness, of love blazed briefly and was

gone just as quickly.

The just man shook his head in confusion. What was that all about?

Then he suddenly felt a terrible pain in the area of his heart. With a stifling cry he held his chest. The void, left by the just heart, was pulsing. It was an open wound that now began to close gradually. The pain was getting worse and worse.

'What the hell...?' said the just man and could barely breathe.

Heavy-going he got up from his bed, left his couch and, bent in pain, he slogged along to the window to open it and let fresh air in. Only with great difficulty did the just man succeeded and greedily he sucked in the fresh cool night air. The stabbing pain became better, but it did not completely disappear. A chest tightness remained in him and so the just man had to fight his way through the night with pain. For a long time he found no sleep, he thrashed around on the right side and then on the left side of his couch.

Hour after hour passed and at four o'clock in the

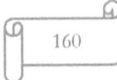

morning it got on top of the just man. With headaches, chest and limbs pains he finally got up and dressed. He wanted to drown the pain in drink at the crack of dawn in the hope that things would be better then.

He stepped out of his room and discovered that his housekeeper had not yet got up. So the just man slipped out of the house with stitches in his chest and disappeared through the streets.

No breath of wind, no noise, no human soul was found outside. Only the street lighting showed the just man the way and was the light in the darkness.

But whoever does what is true comes to the light. Therefore be careful lest the light in you be darkness. If then your whole body is full of light, having no part dark, it will be wholly bright, as when a lamp with its rays gives you light.

Suddenly the just man jerked to a halt.

Those words...

Words like that again...

Wherefrom did he know them?

Shocked, he stared at the emptied dark street. He swallowed hard. His chest stitched, pounded, burned.

The just man continued to walk with distorted pain. These words echoed in his head. What was their meaning?

Not long and the just man reached a bench where men were already sitting and roaring at each other with bottles in their hands. When they recognized the just man, they laughed out loud and shouted: 'Well, who do we have here? Our dearest man on board!'

Loud roaring followed. Immediately he was also given a bottle of high-proof alcohol. 'Drink!' one commanded. 'You'll feel better. No matter what suffering you have.' The just man immediately put the bottle on his lips and greedily poured the contents of the bottle into his mouth. 'Do you feel like another adventure?' one of the men asked the just man and grinned. 'Who are we going to finish somebody off today? Then you should do it this time, you've seen how it works.' Diabolically, he grinned at the just man.

'I just want to get drunk. Thank you,' the just man replied, emptying his bottle and taking a second one from the men while he put the empty bottle on the bench.

The men were roaring.

'Oh, come on. There's nothing to it. It's just a human being that is worthless. Who cares if a person is more or less in the world?' laughed one of the men.

'The world economy,' the just man replied. The men laughed out loud.

Truly, truly, I say to you, everyone who practices sin is a slave to sin.'

The men fell silent. 'What? What was that?' laughed one of them. They gave the just man a challenging look who stood there thunderstruck and expressionless with the bottle in his hand.

He didn't know what he was talking about. Where did these words come from? From what part of his body?

'Why do you not understand what I say? It is because you cannot bear to hear my word. You are of your father the devil, and your will is to do your father's desires. He was a murderer from the beginning,' it came out of the mouth of the just man.

The men looked at each other enraged.

'What the hell are you talking about, man? Who are you?

I thought you were one of us, letting it all hang out, want to experience adventures. We don't need a stupid know-it-all in our squad! Stick to our rules or get lost!'

Furiously the man stood in front of the just man who did not know where these words came from, what they meant, what all this was supposed to mean.

He stood there thunderstruck.

Without any reaction.

'Can you dig it?!' the man hissed in front of him. His eyes were full of anger.

None of them noticed the man behind the thick tree at the bench who was listening and watching them all. The just man was part of the gang that killed this homeless guy?

Stunned the man behind the tree was staring at the scene that occured to him.

Now everyone in the group stepped up to the just man, who still showed no emotion.

At any moment a huge bomb would go off, thought the man behind the tree and already in front of his mind's eye he saw the just man lying dead in a pool of blood on the ground.

The men came closer and closer and the next moment they stormed upon the just man and beat him, kicked him, spat at him, smashed all the empty bottles on him. Until he laid down motionless.

They let up on him, believing he was dead, and ran away.

Quickly the man came out behind the tree, bent over the just man and felt his weak pulse.

* * *

The just man opened his eyes clumsily, laboriously and slowly.

Where was he? Everything was white. Was he dead? Everything was quiet. Where in the heck was he?

Slowly and with pain he turned his head to the side.

There was a strange man sitting reading a book. But soon he looked up and discovered that the just man had awakened. The stranger smiled.

'There you are,' he said kindly, standing up from his

chair by the window and walking towards the just man in his bed.

'You were talking in your sleep,' the stranger added kindly.

The just man looked at him confused. 'Talking?'

The stranger nodded. 'Yes. A name. From a woman. Who was she?'

The just man thought about it. 'I don't remember.'

The stranger nodded seriously. 'I see.'

The just man swallowed. 'Where am I?' he whispered strengthlessly.

'At the hospital. You were beaten up. You slept a few days. Luckily, they were able to restore you. You were badly hurt.' The stranger looked pityingly at him. Immediately the memory returned and the just man sighed.

'It was this gang...,' the strange man began. He now sat down on a chair next to the bed of the just man.

'May I ask you a question?'

The just man looked at the strange man confused, but

nodded.

The stranger was clearing his throat. 'Well... this gang... what are you of all people being up against them?'

Fourteen

The just heart waved the ship's troop goodbye. They could let him out somewhere in between. It was still far from home...

For a long time it looked after the ship that was more and more fading. All at once it was all alone.

It was daytime and people were running around everywhere. Many hearts walked along the path and looked upon the just heart full of malice.

This ignored their evil and smiled kindly back. Scared by this unexpected reaction, the evil hearts looked away with narrow eyes.

With cheerful disposition the just heart went its way and didn't really know which way to take to get back home. Did it ever find its way home?

He missed his master.

It doesn't bear contemplating how things are going for him right now without his heart! What kind of evil deeds he had committed so far? The just heart sniffed with sadness. It was all his fault. Why did it have to be so foolish and think that it would be nicer elsewhere and that it would be better to live there? Why hadn't it listened to its master? Now it had plunged him into a terrible evil life, from which he will probably never again find out and die as an evil old man. Its master wanted to be such a good man and die as a just man. And because of his stupid foolish heart, he was prevented from doing so!

The just heart stopped and sadly watched the hustle and bustle on the streets. So isn't it not surprising that people voluntarily took their hearts out of their chests so that it didn't put a spoke in their wheel in their plans for their lives?

No.

Now the just heart was no longer surprised.

Now it knew the answer.

But would it still be worthwhile to return to its master now, where everything has already been lost?

The just heart sent a heavy sigh heavenwards and stood lonely and sad on the street.

What had to be done now?

Everyone advised him to return.

But was that really the answer?

The just heart walked along the road, further and further and further. Stunned with sadness, guilty conscience and pain, it lost itself in thoughts and didn't even realize how far it had already gone. There was no longer any hustle and bustle, but rather creepy silence.

Then the just heart was frightened and stopped dead in its tracks.

It looked around.

It seemed like a ghetto to him.

Everything was dark, dirty and neglected.

Suddenly he heard loud roaring voices and screams.

They approached. And suddenly it saw a horde of hearts — dark, pitch-black and full of leprosy.

Viled language filled the yard and the just heart was frightened by these words, which these hearts uttered, for the just heart had never heard such words before.

The hearts began to beat and spit on each other and even drew out weapons.

Once again, the just heart was terrified.

What happened here? Why did hate rage between them?

So the just heart stepped towards them and shouted

through the noise: *'Men, you are brothers. Why do you wrong each other?'*

Here one of the hearts jostled it away and screamed: *'Who made you a ruler and a judge over us?'*

And the other one shouted angrily: 'So what do you want us to do, huh?' He laughed diabolically.

The just heart said to them: *'Do not extort money from anyone by threats or by false accusation, and be content with your wages!'*

Then all the evil hearts laughed and the just heart stood there without emotion. Suddenly—without any warning—one of the hearts striked the just heart brutally in the face.

Everybody laughed.

The just heart was lying on the ground holding its face in pain.

In agony, it was laboriously re-erecting itself and everyone stared at it unbelievingly. Then the just heart took its hands off his bleeding face and said: *'If what I said is wrong, bear witness about the wrong; but if what I said is* right, why do you strike me?'

Silence.

Nobody said a word.

Scared, they were staring at the just heart.

'Who the hell are you?' whispered a black heart and stared badly at the just heart.

'Save yourselves from this crooked generation!' the just heart only said. 'Why do the nations rage, and the peoples imagine a vain thing? The kings of the earth set themselves, and the rulers take counsel together, against the Lord.'

That's when the bad hearts started laughing again.

'Ooh, he's talking about God!' roared one of the hearts.

'Don't give us that fiddlesticks, all right? Stop it and go!'

The just heart smiled mildly.

'Whether it is right in the sight of God to listen to you rather than to God, you must judge.'

The evil hearts grinned spitefully.

'But my answer is this: We must obey God rather than men.'

Again the evil hearts were laughing.

'Take care of yourselves, otherwise you might even be

found opposing God. '

Then one of the hearts — the one that had beaten the just heart in the face — stepped forward and grinned badly at the just heart.

'Do you have sacred things to return to everything we say?' He laughed evil.

The just heart smiled mildly. *'Peace be with you. '*

The evil heart flashed its eyes furiously at it.

'People and their hearts *should seek God,'* the just heart began, *'perhaps feel their way toward him and find him. Yet he is actually not far from each one of us, for 'In him we live and move and have our being'; as even some of your own poets have said, 'For we are indeed his offspring.' The times of ignorance God overlooked, but now he commands all people everywhere to repent. '*

With love the just heart looked at the evil heart. This one swallowed. Tears of rage filled his eyes.

'You know what?' the evil heart hissed. 'Your oh, great God has done all this to me. Look at my wounds! Your God hates me, why else am I so bad?'

The just heart looked at it with pity and sighed.

'It's not about hate. Your pain exists, *because it is for the glory of God, so that God may be glorified through it.* The problem is that everyone thinks suffering is a punishment. You did something you have to pay for. But it can't be, because otherwise it would be distributed very unfairly. And if it is, then you will not have to pay more than others on earth. A wise old heart once told me, just before his passing away, that suffering burns out evil, sin and it is actually an honour that God makes you suffer so much because he has set a special hope in this person and in no way wants it to be lost. So with all the suffering, you're more special than hated. God doesn't want you to get lost and your master. Suffering shall chastise you and all evil shall burn out of you. It hurts, yes, but it heals. Like medicine that doesn't taste good, but heals all the better than medicine that's tasty and has no effect.'

The evil heart eyeballed the just heart speechlessly, as did all the others. Big eyes stared at the wise, just heart. 'Are you serious?' asked the evil heart full of tears in the eyes.

The just heart nodded. 'Yes, my son. Just believe it.'

It looked at the evil heart with love, which now began to understand. The other hearts also seemed to understand.

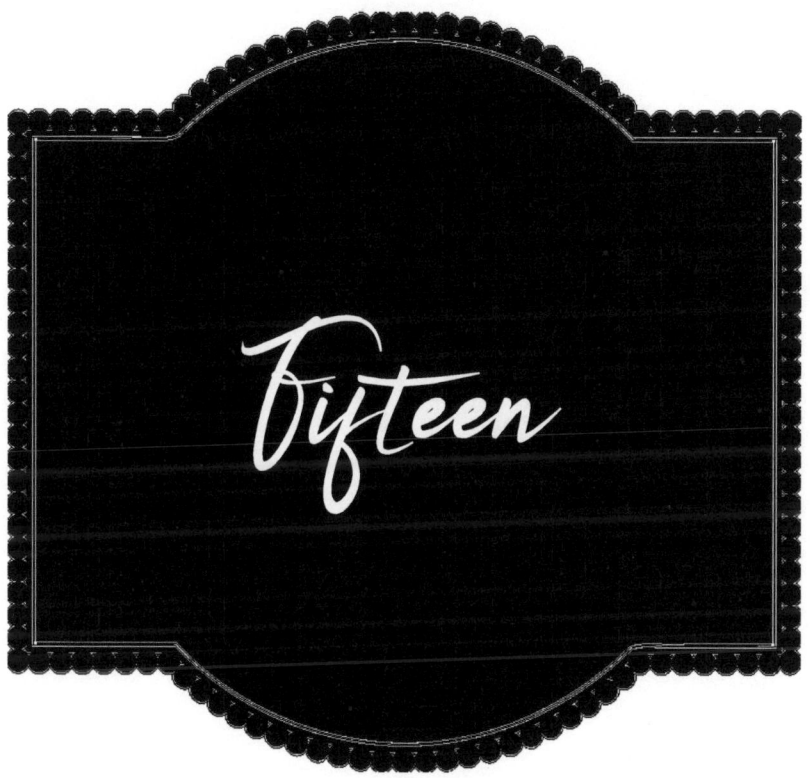

'What actually happened,' the just man wanted to know from the stranger.

He looked at the just man a little tormented. 'Well... you've been beaten up by this gang. They thought you were dead and so they ran away. I watched everything behind that big tree at the bench.'

The just man looked at the stranger expressionlessly. 'So you've also heard ... everything?'

The stranger nodded. 'I'm afraid so.'

The just man sighed.

'But listen, I won't tell anyone if you don't want to. It is your conscience and you must know when the time has come.'

'I don't think I have a conscience anymore,' the just man replied.

The stranger looked at him seriously. 'What happened to you?'

The just man took a deep breath. He shook his head.

'I don't know. From one day to the next, all at once I became a different person. Like I've lost my heart. I don't understand.'

The stranger kept looking at him seriously.

Silence.

The just man now looked at the stranger in composure.

'Why did you help me? After all I've done and all I've become.'

The stranger cleared his throat. 'I've always been a great admirer, you know. I admired your manner. Your warmness: how you embrace life, how you accept everything—no matter what—with all your heart and how you make the best of everything. How to strengthen the weak, nourish the poor, dress the naked, take in the homeless. How you meet the bad world with the good as a sword. I've always admired that about you, my dear.' Strong-willed, the stranger looked the just man in his face.

This one swallowed hard. 'And now you do not anymore ...,' he concluded.

'Oh yes,' it shot out of the stranger, 'oh yes. That's why I'm here. Because I want to give you a leg-up. Because I won't drop you, I won't give up on you. After all these years, I've learned one thing from your teachings: to right each other. Over and over again, as often as necessary. This is the way to the world we all long for, this is the only way to peace, to true life here on earth. A man among men, all at the same level, no one weak, poor, small, outcast. I learned that, my good man, from you and now I want to keep it that way myself,' said the stranger to the just man and breathed heavily after these strong words.

The just man stared at him with wide eyes. 'What you're talking about,' he began, 'seems so ... strangely familiar.'

Now the stranger seemed confused. 'I beg your pardon?'

The just man stared at the stranger. 'I can barely remember ... how I had once been.'

It was almost a whisper.

The stranger looked the just man straight in the eye. 'There is something strange going on here,' he concluded, and his expression became hard.

The just man looked at the stranger. 'What do you

mean?'

'I think it's very strange that at a moment's notice your heart just seems to have changed into stone. But the strangest thing is that you don't remember who and what you were some time ago. Do you understand? This is too weird. That's not possible!'

Confused, the stranger stared at the just man.

He was now angry.

'Is that supposed to mean you're calling me a liar?!'

He almost screamed it. His eyes became two narrow slits and his lips also narrowed. He breathed heavily.

The stranger was shocked and jumped up from the chair.

'No, I'm sorry, that's not what I meant. It should not be an reproach or even an accusation...'

'Then what the hell do you mean, for God's sake!' the just man shouted.

The stranger swallowed scaredfully. His breath went fast.

Out of hateful eyes, the just man stared at the stranger.

For a long time both stared at each other, the stranger did not dare to say even one word.

'I forgive you', the stranger finally said, 'because you don't know what you're doing.'

The just man was horrified. 'These words...'

The stranger approached the just man again. 'Those are your words, my friend. Your teachings you have got from your God. And which you teach others.'

The just man stared at the stranger with his mouth open. He was speechless.

Silence filled the room. Unspoken thoughts laid in the air of the room, hiding in every corner of the room, haunting through the walls.

The unspoken wafting around endlessly, lying between the two men like moist, heavy, tropical air.

'Where is my heart?' whispered the just man. 'Where is it?'

He looked desperately at the stranger, who now looked at him pityingly.

'Your heart is in your chest,' said the stranger. 'It's still there. It was never gone.' The stranger sat down on the bed, very close to the just man and laid his hand on his chest.

'See, that's where your heart is. Do you feel how it beats?'

Hot, thick tears were running down the cheek of the just man and landed on the hand of the stranger.

Full of pity he looked the just man into the wet, red eyes, which got filled more and more with tears.

The just man sniffed. He shook his head. 'No. It's gone. Can't you feel it?'

More tears dropped onto the hand of the stranger.

'I feel something throbbing. It's your heart.' The stranger smiled at the just man.

Again he shook his head. 'No. Not the heart. It's the stone.'

The stranger sighed. 'My friend. You need rest. Time-out. I'm here. You are not alone.'

The just man swallowed down more tears.

'So what are we going to do now?' he asked.

The stranger was thinking. 'You'll get well, you'll be released, you'll stay with me for a while, and you'll calm your tormented, thorny heart.'

'And then?'

The stranger was confused. 'What ... ?'

'Then what happens next? Nothing's the same anymore and I'm a murderer.'

The just man breathed heavily.

'Well... we'll deal with that soon. First of all, get back on your feet, my friend.'

The stranger smiled.

The just man nodded.

'Terrible what's happening to me right now.'

The stranger looked at him pityingly.

'Yes. It is. And together we will find out why. What exactly is behind it. Worst of all, you don't even remember who you were before you became what you are. Isn't that strange? It's like as if a demon jumped into your soul. As if he carried away all your memories and all the good.'

A mooth summer breeze flew through the bushes and riled up the leaves. These were one of the few draughts that the wind did these days, because the air was wafting with heat and almost burned the grass, which had already turned into hay.

The house of the just man had recently been abandoned, only darkness reigned in it. Since the just man had freed this from all the books and more so long ago, the darkness now seemed to dwell in it.

The housekeeper had moved back into her own little house and could now let her mind and spirit rest a little since the day the just man was so warmly welcomed by this stranger in his home.

But inside the just man it was not as summerly warm and bright as the regiment of summer with all its glory yielded.

Emptiness, desire and darkness reigned in the just man's chest. With empty black eyes he sat there in the stranger's living room, staring spellbound at the wall.

He whispered something.

A name.

Gently the stranger entered his living room and listened to the quiet words of his new friend. That name again. Of this woman...

The stranger approached the just man and sat next to him on the chaise longue. The housekeeper of the just man had advised the stranger to try it with good chocolate biscuits and a hot cup full of chocolate. So the stranger sat next to the just man and held a tray full of soul pleasures in his hands. 'Brother,' the stranger whispered to the just man, 'may you partake of something? It makes you happy again.'

The just man turned his head to the tray on the stranger's knees. Then he turned his head to the wall again and whispered: 'If you have no heart anymore, it is impossible to ever be happy again. Not truly.'

The stranger swallowed. 'Why are you talking like that? Your heart is in your chest, where else would it be?'

The just man did not seem to react, but then he whispered: 'It has gone away. The cup of sorrow was just too bitter.'

The stranger gave the just man a serious-looking for a long time. He didn't know what to think. He wondered if the just man had gone mad. Shouldn't he take him to a house of correction rather than keep meddling with him himself?

No.

The stranger thought highly of the just man and also of his teachings. If he really was a follower and admirer, he had to prove it, to live it himself.

Otherwise you wasn't a follower.

Just to say yes and amen did not make a saint out of a disciple. Works were important. Love.

So the stranger placed the tray on the small side table next to the chaise longue and took a deep breath.

'If you want something to eat or drink,' he said, 'it's right here. Try it. It feels very good. You know it.'

With these words the stranger left the just man and left him to his sadness.

* * *

The days passed and the just man left himself completely
to his gloom.

The stranger watched this tragedy for weeks.

He was heartbroken.

What could he do for his new friend?

One day he entered the living room — in which the just
man had been thinking gloomy thoughts since the day he
arrived in this house on the chaise longue — , standing
next to the just man. The stranger sat down gently next to
him and saw that his friend had cried again. He sat there
numb and stared at the opposite wall with an idle glance,
as he already used to do for weeks.

When the stranger sat next to him, he showed no
emotion.

The environment and all the people in it had become
completely unimportant to the just man. He didn't care
about himself.

The stranger cleared his throat.

'Who is this woman,' he began whispering, 'whose name
you keep whispering?'

He waited.

It seemed as if the just man had not heard him. But the stranger knew that he had heard it. Only the gloom slowed down every reaction of the just man and so it took a little while until he turned his head to his new friend and looked at him out of painful eyes.

The stranger looked back with heartbreaking concern.

The just man swallowed down some tears before answering quietly: 'She is the woman who possessed my heart and whose heart I have killed.'

A tear rolled down his cheek and his head turned back to the wall.

The stranger swallowed hard. 'A-and... what happened to her?'

It was little more than a whisper, quieter than the stranger had intended and he almost feared that the just man had not heard him. He just wanted to launch into a repeat of the question, the just man replied aloud: 'I killed her!'

The stranger was frightened. Both for the volume and the information it contained.

'What do you mean, you killed her?' the stranger asked.

'How?'

The just man cried bitterly. He sobbed.

'She had loved me so much. So much. But I didn't give her enough to make her heart happy and complete. She wrote me desperate letters that only reached me after her death. I killed her. Her heart died of thirst because of me. Because of me, she no longer had the will to live. Because of me her heart stopped.'

After these words violent convulsions attacked the just man and a hot flood of tears broke out.

The stranger was even more frightened. 'But ... my friend! Calm down!' he called out in panic and jumped up.

The just man was laying — writhing in mental pain — on the ground and screamed.

'Let me die!' he cried. 'Just let me die!'

The stranger fell into despair and crouched next to the just man to calm him down.

'Calm down!' he shouted. 'Wake up.'

But all efforts were in vain.

The just man fell into his psychically deep black hole and

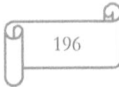

there seemed to be no way out.

With hands and feet the stranger tried to calm his friend, who struggled, screamed and cried like a man possessed on the ground.

'Kill me!' the just man cried. 'Please! Kill me!'

The stranger shook his head heavily. 'Never!'

The just man screamed and shouted even more violently. 'I must die! I have no right to live when she's dead because of me!' That's how the just man screamed.

He was flailing and suddenly he and the stranger found themselves in a wild and bloody duel.

They wrestled with each other, and loud roarings and the falling down of some furniture filled the room.

After what seemed like an eternity it was over and the just man and the stranger laid bleeding on the ground.

A star-bright cool night covered the streets. A black blanket of stars cloaked houses, trees, streets in peaceful sleep.

The earth was lying there quiet and peacefully. Nothing indicated that at that moment there were famines, torture, wars, hatred going on somewhere in the world. As if the game had been interrupted for a few hours for a modicum of sleep, as playing children do: If the mother calls for dinner, the children put their game aside; during this break they are again as good as friends to continue their game afterwards, until the bed calls to sleep, to interrupt the game again and pretend as if nothing had happened during the game.

Like it was all just a game.

As if the world could put aside and take up evil at any time, take up the war and put it aside again, famine, death, just as it pleases.

As if the world were a huge playground ... and as if every person were just playing and none of it was meant seriously ... as if wars or death were a game.

So the just heart walked through the dark streets and alleys of the night, still trying to finally find home.

Suddenly something was moving a few meters away in front of him. Or someone?

It was too dark to see anything.

The just heart walked boldly closer.

Only when it stopped under a street lamp did it realize that it was — also standing under a lamp — another heart.

But of a color the just heart had never seen before. It was dark brown. Like chocolate! Like that his master loved to drink and who enlivened his spirit!

The just heart was surprised.

What kind of heart was this one?

From afar it heard loud shouts. They didn't sound very nice and diabolical laughter was following.

'Something like you deserves to be killed! But rejoice, Negro — nothing will happen to you today!'

Another diabolical laugh followed.

Then the voices faded, leaving behind soft whimpering and sobbing.

Immediately pity attacked the just heart and it

approached closer to the dark figure cowering on the floor under the street lamp.

The just heart sat down next to this.

With a face distorted with pain, the just heart looked at the dark brown sad and crying little heart and gently laid one hand on his head.

The little heart was terrified dreadfully.

Shock was truly written in his face.

The just heart smiled mildly. 'Peace be with you, my son. You have nothing to fear from me. I'm not going to hurt you.'

With a soft, warm, calm voice it spoke to the frightened little heart on the floor.

This looked suspiciously at the just heart. 'What do you want from me?'

The just heart continued to smile mildly. 'Helping you.'

The little heart seemed surprised. 'Helping? Me? Why?'

The just heart was now surprised as well. 'Why not, then? People seem mad at you. Tell me why.' Friendly and cheerfully it smiled at the little heart.

'I'm a Negro. That's why they're angry with me.'

'A Negro?'

The just heart did not really know what to think of this word.

It did not know this.

The little heart nodded. 'Yes. That's what they call me and my own kind. We have the wrong color.'

'The wrong color?'

The just heart was unable to make tail of the fact that there was something like a wrong skin color. Who prescribed such a thing?

The little heart looked sad. It nodded.

Suddenly the evil voices returned. The little heart was startled.

'Help,' it begged the just heart.

This one looked at the poor heart determined and strong.

'I am with you,' it said.

Finally, three deep black hearts stood in front of the little heart and the just heart and looked at them spitefully.

'Uh-huh, look, Negro has found an ally!'

Stupid laughter followed.

'Tell me, do you realize that as a clean person you should not keep company with unclean people? With dirt?'

Even more stupid laughter followed.

The just heart looked pityingly at the three evil hearts.

'You are those who justify yourselves before men, but God knows your hearts. For what is exalted among men is an abomination in the sight of God. And also what is an abomination in the sight of men, for God it is exalted,' the just heart spoke calmly.

The evil hearts became silent. Confused they looked at the just heart.

'The good person out of the good treasure of his heart produces good, and the evil person out of his evil treasure produces evil, for out of the abundance of the heart his mouth speaks,' thus the just heart kept speaking and the little heart by its side looked at it full of amazement and admiration for its words.

The just heart, however, faced the evil hearts composed, but yet mildly.

'You cleanse the outside of the cup and of the dish, but inside you are full of greed and wickedness. You fools! Did not he who

made the outside make the inside also? But give as alms those things that are within, and behold, everything is clean for you. For you tithe mint and rue and every herb, and neglect justice and the love of God. These you ought to have done, without neglecting the others. Woe to you! For you are like unmarked graves, and people walk over them without knowing it. For you load people with burdens hard to bear, and you yourselves do not touch the burdens with one of your fingers. What God has made clean, do not call common! God has shown me that I should not call any person common or unclean.'

The just heart looked at the evil hearts without any expression.

They stared back with confusion and suspicion.

There was silence between them all.

The little heart watched heavily breathing, what would probably be following.

Then one of the evil hearts cleared his throat and said with subliminal amusement: 'So you want to say that all are holy and pure and that negro here is like all of us? Is that correct?'

He stepped arrogantly closer to the just heart. This one

nodded.

'Yes. That's right. *God shows no partiality, but in every nation anyone who fears him and does what is right is acceptable to him.'*

The evil heart — now standing right in front of him — looked at the just heart with a chuckle. 'Ho-hum.'

It sized the just heart up from top to bottom, but this one kept speaking unwaveringly: *You know that those who are considered rulers of the Gentiles lord it over them, and their great ones exercise authority over them. But it shall not be so among you. But whoever would be great among you must be your servant, and whoever would be first among you must be slave of all. For everyone will be salted with fire. Salt is good, but if the salt has lost its saltiness, how will you make it salty again? Have salt in yourselves, and be at peace with one another.'*

The evil hearts looked at each other. It was hard to say what exactly they were thinking, because now there was no expression on their faces.

'Beautiful words,' one of the hearts finally said.

'Unfortunately, that's all! You are a traitor who unites

himself and bother with all the scum of the world! Don't you have any pride? Bloody blood traitor!' The evil heart were hissing it. 'Here we are the ones who keep everything clean and watch out for decency. You should insult negroes like that—not us!'

The just heart laughed softly. 'I'm not insulting anyone.'

Then it continued: *Those who are well have no need of a physician, but those who are sick.'*

The evil heart rumbled from the depths of his body.

'A color is a color,' the just heart elaborated on its thoughts. 'A form is a form. A size is a size. That alone cannot form a character, a nature. What can we say about your nature? Your color, shape, size seems generally and socially speaking perfect, pure. But what about your inner self? Are you ready to be perfect inside too? Or is it just your appearance? Superficial things are easy to find and they enrapture. But gold you have to dig out and has much more value. But what if they dig with you? Will they find gold there? Or just bitumen?'

'Let it be,' said the just heart, 'it won't make your life any better.'

It looked urgently at the evil hearts, who now stared back with frosty looks.

'Well,' said one of the hearts, 'for now. But there will be consequences, I swear. At least, you have not converted us with your gibberish. For we carry on what we believe in.'

The three black hearts turned around and disappeared into the darkness of the night.

The just heart smiled torturedly.

He felt sorry for them and was sad at the same time because of their hardness.

The little heart looked gratefully at the just heart. 'Thank you, my friend, for being by my side. That you dislodged them without violence.'

His little eyes were glowing with joy.

The just heart smiled mildly back and opened its arms.

The little heart and the just heart now were lying in each other's arms like brothers and were shining amicably for the world like a light in the wicked darkness.

Then the little heart let go of the just heart and asked with a smile: 'Where are you from? Where is your home?' The just heart now looked sad. 'I'm afraid I can't say, for I don't know the name of the place. Nobody's ever been able to get me home. I think I'm lost forever. My master remains heartless and dies in shame.' It stood there downcasted and the little heart looked at the just heart full of sorrow.

'Brother, my master is still in his bed. In the morning, however, he leaves for another place for his trading operations. Then come with us and see if this is the place of your home,' this one spoke and looked at the just heart hopefully.

His face immediately brightened. 'But... where am I going to sleep?'

The little heart laughed. 'Well, with me and my master. Come on, I'll take you there.'

So the just heart and the little heart went hand in hand to his home in the darkness of the night.

The moon stood high in the sky, guarding all the human

children who slept under the dark blanket of the nightly sky and drifted through the gates of dreams to other worlds, so that all those travelers could return safe and sound in the morning when the sun replaced the moon in its watch.

Soon they reached the home of the little heart and its master, who slept in his bed and slumbered joyfully.

The just heart looked at the master of the little heart and smiled. So gently was this man sleeping, his breath was calm and true peace was lying on his face.

How much pain had this person already endured, since all other people used to believe that dark was a wrong skin color?

How full was his cup of sorrow?

And how bitter did it taste?

The just heart swallowed when it saw a few deep scars on this man's face through the dimly moonlight shining through the room window. He was beaten very often. His body. His heart. And yet the little heart remained in his master's chest faithfully devoted and hopeful.

A thrust went through the just heart. It felt so guilty. So

cowardly.

What right has the just heart ever had to believe that it deserved no suffering and would have to leave to escape it?

What was the right of others? Did they have a chance to escape? Not to drink the cup of sorrow?

Who had the right to wish for a more care-free life when there were people who fared so much worse than you? No one can ever escape. None.

The just heart swallowed. His eyes were filling with tears.

The just heart had acted unjustly.

* * *

'Stand up, brother! We have to go!'

The little heart shook the just heart to wake it up.

Only with difficulty he got his eyes open and had to orientate himself first.

When the memory came back, the just heart shot up and stared at the little heart expectantly and smiling. 'All right, let's not waste any time.'

Immediately they jumped behind the master of the little heart onto his vehicle and the just heart looked at this person more closely. He was scarred by suffering, no question. It would have loved to help this poor man. Too happy to end his suffering. Too much to change the hearts of men on this earth so that small-minded thinking could no longer find its way.

Then the just heart saw that this person smiled and was happily whistling away to oneself every now and then. The just heart got wide eyes. There were just a few of these kind of people. Despite suffering, beatings, insults or even death threats — his faith, his love, his hope was the source of his strength.

And that in turn produced strength again in order to obtain even more strength.

He watched the master of the little heart with awe. And then the little heart itself. It also smiled just as joyfully as if it would have huge fun today. When only evil was waiting to ruin it ...

The journey led over muddy dirt tracks, over bumpy

cobblestones, over bumpy stone paths.

It seemed to take an eternity and the just heart was very afraid that it would only end up in a strange city again, where it had to see once more how it came home.

'Tell me, my brother,' the just heart started, 'how much longer, do you think, will it take?'

The little heart smiled. 'I think it won't be far now. We've driven a lot and come a long way. And so far we have been lucky that no robbers or other bad people have attacked our vehicle. In generel, it will be not well-received to see a black man driving a vehicle and driving around as a trader. The general opinion of our kind is, that we are only useful either as slaves and servants or better we were completely dead.'

The little heart looked sad.

The just heart sighed compassionately.

Do not fear those who kill the body, and after that have nothing more that they can do. Fear him who, after he has killed, has authority to cast into hell.'

It smiled cheerfully at the little heart.

'There is no wrong skin color, there is only wrong

thinking,' it went on.

This one smiled back. 'You're a sweet heart, brother. You're so kind to me, I rarely experience that. And you are so wise.'

The just heart smiled lovingly. 'I got it from my master. He doesn't care about the shell — the core is important. He's always about the core. He doesn't care about anything else.'

The little heart got wide eyes. 'Who's your master, brother?'

The just heart told the little heart about his famous master, how he lived, how he was. Only good things he could tell about him.

Finally, the little heart looked at the just heart in shock. 'What is it, my brother?' the just heart wanted to know full of sorrow.

The little heart swallowed. 'This man you're talking about is known throughout the country. He was it — as you surely know — already before, because of his kindness and mercy. But the story of his new coldness and heartlessness also did the rounds. I already sensed that you were his missing heart, but I wasn't sure,' the little heart began. 'Your master is generally blamed on having committed a murder.'

The just heart stared stiffly at the little heart. It didn't understand what it was saying.

'And that one whom he had murdered was my master's brother.'

The just heart was incapable of any movement.

'No,' it breathed stunned. 'Oh, no!'

'Oh, yes,' the little heart replied. It was deeply concerned. 'My master knows of your master as his brother's murderer. He has not yet been arrested because no evidence has been found that he actually did so and also because he has disappeared. But when my master meets your master ... I don't know what he'll do.'

The little heart looked at the just heart in panic.

'Maybe he will look for your master when he arrives in your place! Find him best first,' said the little heart, 'so that he has the opportunity to act with heart.'

Thus they were lying there — the just man and the
stranger; breathless, wheezing, bleeding, exhausted.
The stranger slowly picked himself up. He stood above
the just man, held down one hand and said: 'Well fought,
brother. But now — peace!'
Breathless, he looked at the just man and waited for a
reaction. He looked at the stranger without any
expression and hesitantly seized his hand, whereupon he
helped the just man with a jerk back on his feet.
'So you're really serious about it,' the just man began,
and the stranger looked at him confused, 'about giving
me a leg-up.'
The just man winked with a grin.
The stranger understood and began to laugh out loud.
'Yes!' he shouted. 'Yes, that's right!'
Now the just man also laughed and both were suddenly
in each other's arms. Then the just man freed himself
from the hug, looked closely at the stranger and said:
'You really look bad, friend!'
He grinned.

The stranger laughed. 'Oh, thank you very much.'

With it he wiped his blood from his face, while the just man emulated his deeds and also wiped his blood away.

'What do you think: should we again behave like grown-up, civilized people from now on, boring as it may sound?'

The stranger grinned at the just man.

He laughed. 'If I have to.'

The stranger now laughed, too. 'Oh, yes, we have to. Urgently!'

With this he went to the side table of the chaise longue, which was knocked over, put it back in place and said: 'Lucky I didn't bring hot chocolate with me today! That would have been a terrible mess!' He laughed. He looked at the just man who did not laugh, but stared back absent-mindedly.

'Hot chocolate?' he asked.

The stranger nodded. 'Do you want some?'

'Absolutely!'

* * *

'I am home!' said the just heart. 'I am truly back home!'
Radiance laid upon its face and the little heart looked at it
equally cheerful. 'I'm really happy for you. But
remember, brother, try to find your master as soon as
possible, do you hear me?'
The little heart looked at it forcefully, which now nodded
seriously.
'Find out where he had gone underground. Then jump
quickly into his chest,' said the little heart.
'I try my best,' said the just heart. 'Thank you for
everything, my friend.'
The little heart smiled. 'No. I must thank YOU. YOU
were MY help.'
Both looked at each other with a smile. 'May you do
well.'
The just heart nodded and whispered a 'thank you'
before it ran away. At first it ran back to its old house
where it lived. But everything was abandoned. Where

was it supposed to be searching?

Where could he have gone?

It looked around in despair.

It was noon in the meantime, the sun shone brightly down from the sky.

Suddenly the just heart recognized from afar the housekeeper who was talking to someone. An older lady. The just heart approached her.

'No, he hasn't lived there for weeks, my dear,' said the housekeeper.

'Where did he suddenly go? You can't even see him anymore! What happened?' the elderly lady asked curiously.

The housekeeper was looking for some help. 'Oh, nothing special. He is not so well, a stranger has taken care of him. He's staying with him now.'

The elderly lady nodded. 'Ah yes. Who is this stranger? Maybe I know him.'

The housekeeper was thinking. 'No, I don't think so. I didn't know him either. They've only known each other a few months. Since the day he came to the hospital. This man came to see him.'

Hospital?—the just heart thought anxiously and appalled at the same time. He wanted to know more.

But then the two ladies bid each other goodbye and the just heart quickly leapt after the housekeeper.

It went through several narrow dark alleys and further away from the house of the just man. Suddenly the just heart recognized a small house, which the housekeeper was heading for and at which she finally stopped.

She knocked.

Shortly afterwards, a wildly blowzed man with bloody scratches on his face opened the door and the housekeeper was startled.

'What has happened?'

Horrified, she held her hand in front of her mouth.

The stranger smiled. 'Oh, not so bad. We have had a little fight. I'll be all right.'

The housekeeper looked surprised. 'A little fight?'

The stranger nodded. 'Yes. But thanks to your advice on hot chocolate, he's feeling a little better.'

The just heart listened. Hot chocolate?

It immediately stormed right into the middle of the house and felt a strong pull. At the same time, someone in a room cried out loud.

My master!—the just heart thought. That's my master! Hurriedly it hopped into the small living room and discovered the just man there, also wildly blowzed and sitting there with bloody scratches and drinking a hot cup full of good chocolate.

Another pull.

The just man gasped, holding his breast.

The just heart also gasped in pain. Quickly it jumped to its master's chest and it was about to jump into, when it recognized with horror that there was a stone in the place where the just heart should have sat.

What was it supposed to do now?

Was it already too late?

Desperately the just heart looked at the stone throbbing in his master's chest and how he contorted his face with pain. How was his heart supposed to help him now?

The just heart was shocked when it heard a man outside roaring out loud: The master of the little heart! He was here! Had he also followed the housekeeper?

The just heart looked around in panic.

How could he manage to get back into his master's chest in time?

Then all of a sudden the little heart jumped into the room. It saw that the just heart was hesitating. 'What are you waiting for?'

Desperately, it looked at the just heart.

The just heart now wept bitterly.

'I'm too late! He already has a heart of stone!'

Hot tears ran down it face and it sobbed heavily.

Immediately the little heart was with him and saw the stone in the chest of the just man.

'Maybe we can pull it out together, brother,' the little heart said. 'But it will hurt your master like hell. It's already grown strongly together with his flesh.'

It looked at the just heart expectantly. It nodded. 'All right.'

Immediately both hearts reached into the just man's chest and grasped the stone with their hands. They tugged at it hard and the just man screamed. In pain, he dropped the cup of cocoa, which shattered loudly on the floor.

Immediately the housekeeper and the stranger rushed to the door, behind them the master of the little heart.

'My friend, what's wrong?' the stranger shouted in panic. 'Is it your heart?'

Everybody seemed to be in panic.

The just heart and the little heart kept on tugging at the stone with all their might, which could only be moved with difficulty. The just heart felt it slowly tearing off from the flesh of the just man and it overcame him severe nausea.

This painful act hurt the just heart terribly.

It had returned home to make up for everything and instead it had to inflict terrible pain on its beloved master again ...

'What's wrong with you? Please say something! Shall I send for the doctor, take you to the hospital?'

The stranger was out of his head for panic.

The housekeeper was shocked and held her hand in front of her mouth.

The master of the little heart also looked at the spectacle shocked and as pale as death.

The just man was bright red, cold sweat was visible on his head and face, his cries of pain were almost unbearable for everyone involved.

'We've almost made it,' said the little heart hopefully, pulling on the solid stone. The just heart was horror-stricken to hear his master's death cries. This suffering hurt him terribly, as if it were tearing itself into two pieces.

Suddenly the just heart and the little heart held the stone in their hands, which still had parts of the flesh and blood of the just man sticking onto it.

At the very moment when the stone was pulled out of the just man's chest, there was a tremendous jolt and he had no more pain. Without any movement he sat quietly on the chaise longue and stared straight ahead.

Everyone stared at him and waited.

Silence.

'What's the matter with him?' the housekeeper complained quietly. Little tears rolled down her face and she sniffed.

The stranger approached the just man. His eyes were wide open with panic. 'My brother,' he whispered, 'what is happening to you? How can I help you?'

The just heart gave the little heart the stone into the hand and with a leap it sat again in the chest of the just man, his master.

At the same moment the just man breathed heavily, held his chest and groaned.

Again everyone around him panicked.

Then the just man breathed deeply. It was finished.

Hot tears now were running down his face. 'It's back,' he whispered scarcely audible. 'Thank God.'

The stranger looked at his friend desperately. 'What is wrong with you, brother?'

Now the master of the little heart stepped forward. 'I

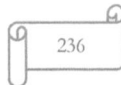

guess that's called justice, huh?' With a cool expression he stood in the middle of the room.

The stranger drew himself up in front of him. 'Excuse me, what do you mean?'

The just man stood up from the chaise longue, reordering his clothes and hair and turned to the man. His countenance bespoke gentleness and pain.

The man, however, angrily flashed his eyes at the just man. 'You!' he started out loud. 'You killed my brother! I know it! It was you!'

The stranger looked at the just man with concern. He knew what was coming. What would happen to his new friend.

The just man returned the look filled with hate of the man with a painful expression. He nodded. 'I guess I am.'

He lowered his head.

The man was perplexed. 'You don't deny it?' With wide eyes he stared at the just man.

He directed his look towards the man again. 'I know

what I've done. And I know I'm guilty. Before God and man.'

The man seemed upset for a few seconds, but immediately picked up courage.

His hate-filled gaze returned. 'Yes. Damn it! You are! Guilty!'

The stranger intervened. 'Please!' he begged. 'Please! He didn't know what he was doing. He wasn't himself, he was exhausted. Besides, he's not the real perpetrator, just the accomplice! The real killer is someone else!'

His gaze was begging.

But the man snorted scornfully. 'And this is supposed to affect me now? My brother is dead! Dead! You got that?'

The stranger swallowed.

The just man lowered his eyelids. His deed affected him very much. The sudden experiences and memories from the journey of his heart were added to that. Everything struck him hard now. But his heart had learned something new and was now beating in his chest with composure and strength.

The just heart smiled at the little heart that smiled back.

It quickly jumped back into its master's chest and he suddenly gasped.

'Please,' the just heart begged to the little heart, 'you know what happened and why. I am guilty, not my master! Let your master act in love.'

Begging, the just heart looked at the little heart.

The little heart nodded seriously. 'I'll do my best.'

The just man did not dare to look at his victim's brother and continued to hold his head and eyelids down.

'Look at me when I'm talking to you!' the man shouted.

A tear ran down the just man's cheek and landed on his shoe. 'I can't,' he whispered. 'I don't dare to look at you.'

The man stared at the just man stunned. He stood there frozen. 'Nothing you do or say will ever bring him back,' said the man with tears in his eyes.

'That's right,' sniffed the just man. 'But I can and will take the punishment and make atonement for your brother. I would be scourged three times a day for the rest of my life if that would make you feel better.'

The man stared desperately at the just man.

'Did you murder him because he was black? Hm?' he looked at him furiously. The just man shook his head.

'No. There will never be reasons for murder. My reason came from somewhere else. Out of sheer heartlessness only.'

More tears filled the man's eyes.

'Please,' the just heart begged again and looked at the little heart in pain. 'Oh, please.'

This one looked back desperately.

Suddenly the man collapsed under tears and cried bitterly.

He emptied his heart, which was still full of grief and sorrow, in the middle of the room next to the housekeeper, the stranger and the just man, and sobbed violently.

The just man slowly approached and crouched down on the floor beside him. His heart was broken. Full of compassion and love, he looked at the man whose suffering he had caused.

'I tell you something now, my brother,' the just man

began, 'I will turn myself in, for I repent deeply. I'm disgusting myself. I'll pay all the blame. If I ever get out of prison again, I want to be your servant. The rest of my life I will stand by you, help you in everything and serve you. All my money will be yours and I will help you in your life, for I know you are poor and already condemned by the world.'

He looked at the man calmly and waited for his reaction. He sobbed. And nodded hesitantly.

'And I will be your slave, your servant. You will rule me and you may scourge me the rest of my life as often as you please. As many times as you think it will atone for your brother's death.'

With watery eyes the just man spoke and smiled gently. 'And if you like, you can also scourge me on my deathbed, for it will never be completely atoned when a loved one is taken from you by another's hand,' he continued and now was breaking out into heavy sobs. An avalanche of tears broke out of him and all his regrets for his deed revealed.

The man now stared at him expressionlessly. He had not

expected such words and such deep regret.

'I know you,' said the man. 'You are known for your kindness and mercy. So why did you kill?'

The just man sniffed. 'It's almost impossible to explain, and no matter what words I use, it will never be comprehensible. But ... I felt like I had lost my heart. Like I was someone else. I wasn't conscious, I didn't know what I was doing.'

He lowered his head and sobbed again.

'Your brother happened to be there. He wasn't chosen. It wasn't his skin color. It wasn't his fault. It was me alone. I was wrong, not him. His very bad luck led him to be at the wrong place at the wrong time. And so me too. But even if I hadn't been there, your brother would still have died, because his real killer would have been there anyway to murder him.'

Now he burst into loud wailing and his cries of pain filled the stranger's living room.

'And why did he do this?' the man wanted to know.

'He said he wanted to free the city from people who just

hang around and live on benches.'

The man looked at the just man seriously. Some tears
rolled down his face.

The just man sobbed.

'I am so sorry ... so infinitely and indescribably sorry ...'

* * *

So it bechanced that the just man was jailed for his
crimes. By reason of complicity in murder.

He was to spend many years there, but since he was not
the main murderer — just accomplice — and the only one
of the gang who had surrendered, he had the hope of
being released prematurely for good conduct.

Year after year passed by. The just man and his heart
studied books day after day, which nourished and
enlivened the spirit. After his misdeed, the just man
never again wanted to say, think or even read a single
bad word.

Moral reading filled his prison cell, which he had alone,

and with a cheerful disposition, knowing that he was rightly imprisoned here, he served his time in prison.

The housekeeper and the stranger visited him quite often and brought new reading for his studies.

One day the just man received a letter from the master of the little heart — the brother of his victim — which surprised him very much.

It said:

My dear fellow,

now several years have passed already, since you took my brother away from me. But your actions and your words and remorse and your voluntary imprisonment do not let me go.

I know you never wanted to kill, I know you're good all through.

Whatever made you to do evil back then, attacked and overwhelmed you like a storm. I know you weren't actively involved in the murder, but passively.

I won't judge you for that any longer.

But since it does not bring my brother back if I hate you and because my dear brother — like me — is a follower of your God's teaching, I would like to tell you today

that I forgive you from the bottom of my heart.
It took a very long time to write this and even more so
to feel it. But forgiveness does not consist of
sugarcoating this act to someone immediately after the
offence, as if nothing had happened. You can come to
terms with it, look at it closely and let it heal ... this
pain.
And then you should reconcile and forgive. Not to
disregard the dead, the offence, the evil. – No. It's to
give peace to yourself. And the other one. Especially
when he's terribly repentant.

I forgive you, my friend, and I greet you with the kiss of
peace!
I bear you no ill will and after your discharge do not
worry, you do not need to become my servant. Go your
way! I think you're hell enough for yourself by knowing
what you've done.
Peace be upon you.

And to put it in your teaching given by your God:

'If your brother sins, rebuke him, and if he repents,
forgive him, and if he sins against you seven times
in the day, and turns to you seven times, saying,
'I repent,' you must forgive him.'